"So," Conner went on, "I'm asking you to talk to her."

In a flash Elizabeth's entire face—no, her entire body—visibly relaxed. And for a split second Conner thought he might have even seen a trace of a smile on her lips. *This is not about you, Liz,* he thought, annoyance shooting through him. *And it's definitely not about us.*

"Of course, Conner," Elizabeth said. "I'd be happy to talk to Megan."

Conner nodded. This was what he had wanted, right? So now he should just thank her and get out of here. "Okay," he mumbled. "Good."

Elizabeth put her hands in her back pockets. She stared back at him for a long moment. Conner felt himself becoming drawn to her, pulled to her. . . . He focused on her sculpted cheekbones . . . on her silver, heart-shaped necklace hanging against her chest . . . on her lips.

Then she opened them to speak, and Conner turned around as quickly as possible. He'd done what he had to do. Now he had to get away. Fast.

"Conner—," he heard Elizabeth call after him, but he was already halfway down the hall.

And he was definitely not going to turn around. No way.

He couldn't trust

did.

Don't miss any of the books in SWEET VALLEY HIGH SENIOR YEAR, an exciting series from Bantam Books!

Visit the Official Sweet Valley Web Site on the Internet at:

http://www.sweetvalley.com

Francine Pascal's SVH senioryear

Bad Girl

CREATED BY
FRANCINE PASCAL

BANTAM BOOKS
NEW YORK · TORONTO · LONDON · SYDNEY · AUCKLAND

RL 6, age 12 and up

BAD GIRL

A Bantam Book / January 2000

Produced by 17th Street Productions,
a division of Daniel Weiss Associates, Inc.
33 West 17th Street
New York, NY 10011.

ISBN: 0-553-49284-5

Published simultaneously in the United States and Canada

Bantam Books are published by Bantam Books, a division of Random House, Inc. Its trademark, consisting of the words "Bantam Books" and the portrayal of a rooster, is Registered in U.S. Patent and Trademark Office and in other countries. Marca Registrada. Bantam Books, 1540 Broadway, New York, New York 10036.

PRINTED IN THE UNITED STATES OF AMERICA

OPM   0 9 8 7 6 5 4 3 2 1

To Marlene Katzman

Elizabeth Wakefield

Change. That's all my life has been about lately. Some of the changes have been horrible—the earthquake, Olivia's death, losing our house, having to deal with some of the more obnoxious El Carro kids.

But I've also gone through some positive changes this year. I've loosened up, had more fun. I've had to grow up a lot, and it was sort of empowering to live apart from my parents for a little while—to be truly independent and make my own choices. I became friends with Tia, Andy, and Angel.

And I fell in love with Conner.

I'm just not sure whether that last change falls under the "good" category or the "bad" one.

Jessica Wakefield

A couple of weeks ago I would've told you that change was the worst thing in the world. I mean, I went from being popular Jessica, queen of the cheerleading squad, life of the party, to the biggest social outcast in southern California.

But looking back, as scary and lonely as it was, my banishment to loserland forced me to realize who my true friends are. And who they're not (ahem, Lila). I've definitely become stronger because of the whole miserable ordeal.

Another thing that made me realize that change can be good was my date with Will this weekend. He took me to this classic burger-and-fries joint in Venice, and after dinner we walked along the boardwalk and drove around the canals and stuff. We had so much fun together — I thought I was going to strain my cheek muscles from laughing so hard.

He's just so cute! Plus there's this insane chemistry between us. And he's so sweet. And cute! Oops . . . Guess I mentioned that already.

Anyway. He makes me feel so incredible. Being with him almost makes everything I went through worth it.

I said <u>almost</u>, okay? I'm not nuts.

TIA RAMIREZ

CHANGE IS WHAT MAKES LIFE EXCITING. SOMETHING HAPPENS—GOOD OR BAD, AND YOU HAVE TO JUST GO WITH IT, SEE WHERE IT TAKES YOU, AND HOP ALONG FOR THE RIDE. THAT'S WHAT LIVING IS ALL ABOUT. I WOULDN'T HAVE IT ANY OTHER WAY.

OKAY, SO IT SUCKS THAT ANGEL IS GONE. HE'S ONLY BEEN GONE FOR TWO DAYS, AND I ALREADY MISS HIM LIKE CRAZY. BUT I'M NOT GOING TO LET IT BRING ME DOWN. NOT FOR A MINUTE. I'M GOING TO HAVE A KILLER SENIOR YEAR. IN FACT, I'M GOING TO GET OUT THERE RIGHT NOW AND HAVE

AN INCREDIBLE DAY. LIVE LIFE
TO THE FULLEST. HAVE FUN.
PARTY!

BUT MAYBE I'LL GIVE ANGEL
A QUICK CALL FIRST. YOU
KNOW, JUST TO SAY HI.

Conner McDermott

Change sucks.

Nothing good ever comes of it. It only makes life more complicated. Even the good changes cause bad things to happen. Need an example? Just look what happened when my mom got convicted of drunk driving and was hauled off to rehab. For a split second I thought she might actually wake up and smell the coffee. Realize she's an alcoholic and deal with it. But Mom's in just as much denial as ever. And to top it off, she asked Gary to stay with us. Just what Megan needs—her deadbeat father to break her heart all over again.

Ken Matthews

A year ago I never thought about change. I never had to. Things were always the same for me. I was Ken Matthews, football star. Olivia's boyfriend. Dumb jock.

Then the earthquake happened, and my entire world was transformed. I didn't see the point in anything anymore. Even living.

Funny thing is, thanks to Maria, things are starting to change for me all over again. I'm actually interested in my classes and want to do well. I've made new friends. And I'm back on my way to being Ken Matthews, football star.

Did I mention that it's all thanks to Maria?

CHAPTER 1
Not a Smiling Matter

Conner McDermott closed his eyes as the hot water pounded against his back. He ran a hand through his dark, wet hair, feeling the steam rise around him.

It was Sunday night, and Conner was normally a morning-shower person. But nothing about Conner's life had been normal lately.

"Or ever," he muttered, turning off the water and stepping out of the shower. He pulled a ratty navy blue towel around his waist, thinking how his lame attempt at relaxing himself had been a total failure. He was still completely keyed up. Which was a familiar feeling for Conner these days.

Sure, he'd managed to escape a little this weekend—by staying far away from his house and his ex-stepfather. He'd practically lived at Tia's, telling her that he wanted to keep her company since Angel had left for Stanford. Tia had probably seen right through him, but Conner didn't care. He just wanted his sanity. Which, at the moment, was nowhere to be found.

Knowing that Gary was in the same house as

him made Conner's entire body tense up. The guy made him sick. If it wasn't for Megan, Conner would have hit the road as soon as Gary moved in.

Megan. Conner's stomach turned. He had barely seen her this weekend. He'd been too busy avoiding home. Meanwhile she was the one who was going to get her heart trampled.

He leaned over the sink, turned on the faucet, and splashed some cold water on his face. Things were going to change. As much as Conner hated to, he had to stick around the house for Megan's sake. She needed him.

Conner picked his faded Levi's off the floor and pulled them on. He scrubbed his face and hair dry, then walked out of the bathroom, heading straight for Megan's bedroom. No time like the present to stick to his resolution. Her door was already open a crack, so he just opened it wider, stepping inside.

"Hey, Megan," he said.

She was sitting cross-legged on the unpolished wooden floor, drawing on a large piece of poster board, felt-tip markers strewn all around her. "Hey!" she said, smiling, her green eyes bright.

Conner knew that Gary was the reason for Megan's smile, but he tried not to think about that. He dropped down onto her iron-frame bed and glanced at the poster board, lifting his head off her ridiculously large array of pillows. "Are you trying to score extra points for an oral presentation or something?"

2

"No!" Megan laughed, pulling her strawberry blond ponytail tighter. "I'm not that much of a kiss butt!" She lifted the poster board up off the floor so Conner could see. "I'm making a welcome-home sign for Mom."

"A what?" Conner sat up straight. In bright, perfect letters Megan had carefully stenciled *Welcome H* and half of a green *o*.

Oh, man. What did she think was going to happen when their mom got home? That their lives were magically going to become better? "That's nice, Sandy," Conner said, using his nickname for her. "But Mom's not coming back for another three weeks."

"I know," Megan responded, placing the poster board back down. "But I can't wait! And I was thinking . . . maybe we could have a little party for her."

Conner moved to the edge of the bed. "A party?"

Megan sat up on her knees, beaming. "Yeah! Just the four of us."

Just the four *of us? Right. Of course.* Megan didn't know about her loving father's mysterious girlfriend—the one Gary was planning on moving into their house.

Conner had always hated Gary. They had done nothing but fight the entire time Gary was married to Conner's mother. And after Gary left, Conner *really* hated him for deserting Megan completely. But a few days ago Conner had learned that Gary had actually fought for custody of Megan—something even

3

Megan herself wasn't aware of. Unfortunately, just when Conner had started thinking his ex-stepfather might be a semiokay guy, he'd overheard Gary inviting his girlfriend to stay. Here. In Conner and Megan's house. While Megan was harboring delusions that her parents would reunite. What a guy.

Shaking his head, Conner stood and walked over to Megan's old wooden bureau. He fiddled with one of the drawer's loose knobs, trying to maintain his cool.

"We could have a nice dinner or something," Megan went on excitedly, oblivious to Conner's reaction. "You know, really make it into a celebration."

Clenching his fists, Conner walked over to her window, swearing that if Gary came in at that moment, he would knock the guy out. Conner narrowed his eyes at the pitch-black sky. Gary had no right to waltz into their life and do this. Get Megan's hopes up. Pretend that he was actually capable of acting like her father.

"Conner?" Megan said. "Is there a reason you're totally spacing?"

Conner sighed and sat down on her white, wooden desk chair. He knew he had to be careful to take the right tone. Otherwise she would just get defensive. She always did when it came to her father. "You gotta realize something, Sandy."

"What's that, O Wise One?" Megan leaned her back against the bottom of her bed, pulling her knees up to her chest.

4

She looked so happy. Conner took a deep breath. "When Mom gets home, Gary is not going to stay. The four of us are not going to be a family."

Megan's eyes became watery in a millisecond. *So much for taking the right tone.*

"This again!" she snapped. "You're only saying that because you don't want it to happen."

"That's not true," Conner argued.

"It is," Megan insisted, standing up, an angry edge to her voice. In quick, jerky movements she began to gather her markers up from the floor. "You hate my father."

Conner looked at the floor. This was going exactly not as planned. Not that he'd had a plan.

He walked over to his sister, picked up a purple marker, and handed it to her. "Megan, this has nothing to do with me. It has to do with Gary."

Megan snatched the marker from him. "Don't, Conner." She shook her head, her cheeks turning pink as they always did when she got upset. "Don't even start with that."

Conner took a step back. "Start with *what*?"

She walked over and threw the markers on her small, white desk, turning her back on him. "Blaming my father. He is my father, you know."

Conner sighed, his frustration mounting. "Yes, Megan. I'm aware of that. But I also know that he—"

"God!" Megan exclaimed, whipping around. "You hate everyone, don't you?"

Conner stared back at her, speechless. He had never seen Megan like this. So full of rage. And at *him*. "What are you talking about?" he finally managed.

Megan grabbed her Nike cross trainers off the floor. She pulled a pair of socks from inside them and stuffed them into her overflowing wicker hamper, then threw the worn-out sneakers onto her closet floor. "I mean, you kicked Liz out of the house—"

"Oh, come on," Conner cut in immediately, his insides contracting at the mention of Elizabeth's name. "We've been over this. That's totally different."

"No, it's not!" Megan picked up her brown teddy bear and tossed it onto her bed. Then she looked at Conner, her eyes narrowed, her cheeks a blotchy red. "You can't get along with anyone, Conner! You're the reason my dad left in the first place."

Conner blinked, feeling like he'd just been slapped. For a moment he simply watched his sister blankly, processing the fact that she *had* actually just uttered those words to him.

Megan stormed back over to her desk, picking up the markers one by one and shoving them into their box. "If you didn't make things so hard for him, if you weren't always cutting school and stealing from the Circle K with Brett and Spencer and all those other losers, he never would've left."

If Conner's body was any tenser, he would have snapped in two. He couldn't believe he was getting blamed for this. Gary deserts his family, but Conner

6

is the villain because he ran with the wrong crowd like *four* years ago? He shook his head. "Is that what he told you?" he asked tersely.

Megan was silent for a moment. She focused on the box of markers. "He didn't have to tell me. . . . I was here," she said quietly.

Conner's head throbbed. He opened his mouth, ready to explode at his sister—but then something made him hesitate.

It was the way she looked as she stood there in her pale blue cotton pajamas, loose strands of knotted red hair falling all around her face. Conner watched as she picked up her stencil and fidgeted with it, her watery eyes cast downward, her lips formed into a pout.

In that instant she looked so vulnerable.

Conner knew that she didn't mean the things she said. She was just sad. And hurt. The person that he *should* blow up at was downstairs—most likely on the phone to his girlfriend.

Without saying another word Conner walked out of her room, closing the door behind him. As he trudged down the hallway, he realized that he'd never felt so hopeless in his life. And it wasn't because Megan's words had stung him—although even he had to admit they had—it was because for the first time in his life, his sister wouldn't listen to him. She was never going to hear what he had to say when it came to her father.

7

Conner reached his bedroom door and was hit by a fresh wave of hopelessness. Because he realized that there was one person out there who Megan *would* listen to. One person she looked up to unconditionally. Elizabeth.

Conner walked into his room, slamming the door behind him.

But hell would freeze over before he'd ask Elizabeth Wakefield for help.

Elizabeth Wakefield stared at the small pink slip that Mr. Collins dropped on her desk in homeroom on Monday morning, speechless. She wanted to lift up the piece of paper, but her muscles seemed to be frozen at the moment. She was speechless *and* paralyzed.

There was no way this slip was for her. Pink slip meant "go to the office." Why would *she* have to go to the office?

This is wrong, Elizabeth thought. *It has to be. He probably dropped it on my desk by accident.*

Then her stomach did a somersault. She noticed that her name was neatly printed on the slip in blue ink. *Her* name. Elizabeth Wakefield. Unbelievable.

"Someone must have made a mistake," Elizabeth muttered, finally regaining control of her body and standing. Pulling down on her short khaki skirt, she marched up to Mr. Collins, who was reading the newspaper at his desk as the rest of the class chattered and finished up their homework, waiting for the bell to ring.

"Mr. Collins," she said. "You don't really think this is for me, do you?"

Mr. Collins glanced up from the paper, his warm brown eyes looking surprised. "Well, it appears to be."

Elizabeth pushed her shoulder-length hair behind her ears. "I know, but I figured that it had to be wrong. . . ."

Mr. Collins was quiet for a moment. Then he began to speak slowly, as if he were choosing his words carefully. "Well, your grades *have* been slipping. And you haven't exactly been on top of the *Oracle* lately."

Elizabeth blinked. She got a C on her last paper, and now she was being sent to the office? How could that be? One C?

"Right." Elizabeth nodded. She twisted her silver necklace around and around her finger. "Okay." She took a step away from his desk, feeling queasy. "So I guess I'll go, then. To the office. Now."

"Right." Mr. Collins nodded, giving her a reassuring smile.

On shaky legs Elizabeth headed for the door. And as she stepped into the eerily tranquil, student-free hallway, she told herself not to panic. She'd been an honor-roll student all her life. She couldn't be in trouble. Maybe the administration wanted to ask her opinion on some school matters or something.

Don't panic, don't panic, Elizabeth chanted to herself as she turned the corner of the hallway and headed straight for the office. *Don't panic, don't panic.* She opened the heavy oak door.

Lydia, the school secretary, was sitting at her perfectly organized desk in the front of the sunlight-filled room, writing in a notebook. Elizabeth didn't really know Lydia, but with her gray hair, soft fuzzy blue sweater, and gold-framed bifocals, she seemed like a nice enough woman. A total grandmother type.

Elizabeth forced a smile. She held out the pink slip with a shaky hand. "Hi," she began. "I'm Elizabeth Wakefield and I—"

"Give that to me," Lydia grunted without looking up. She snatched the pink slip from Elizabeth and grabbed an enormous black binder out from her top desk drawer.

So much for Grandma.

While Lydia flipped through her binder with obvious boredom, Elizabeth bit her lip and studied the Friends Don't Let Friends Drink and Drive poster behind Lydia's head as if it was the most fascinating thing she'd ever seen.

"Here. Elizabeth Wakefield," Lydia announced.

Elizabeth's throat was suddenly devoid of all moisture. Pulling down on the hem of her light blue sweater, she licked her lips. "And?"

Lydia slammed the binder shut. "*And* you're supposed to go see Mr. Valasquez."

A full-fledged circus began a performance inside Elizabeth's stomach. *Mr. Valasquez?* He was Sweet Valley High's guidance counselor. The therapist.

Elizabeth began to sweat.

So much for not panicking.

"Maria! Guess what?"

Maria Slater grabbed her way-too-heavy history textbook out of her locker, then turned to see Ken Matthews jogging up to her. Jogging and *smiling*. Considering that just a few weeks ago he could've won the award for Most Depressed Human on the Planet, it was quite a sight. She smiled back. "What?"

"I just passed Mr. O'Reilly in the hall," he said giddily, rocking forward on the balls of his feet.

Maria laughed, hugging the book to her body. "Okay . . . should I alert the media?"

"Actually, maybe you should." Looking proud, he adjusted his dark blue backpack on his shoulders. "This is kinda newsworthy."

Maria closed her locker with her hip as she stuffed her book into her bag. "Well? Don't keep me in suspense."

"Okay . . ." Ken paused dramatically. "He congratulated me on an excellent paper. He said I did a great job!"

"No way! A compliment from O'Reilly? That's great!" Maria beamed, giving him a quick hug. When she pulled away, she noticed that Ken's cheeks were all flushed. And his blue eyes were practically dancing. It was so cute to see him getting all excited about schoolwork like this. And to think that *she* deserved some credit for Ken's complete one-eighty in attitude . . . that was kind of cool.

"Yeah, well . . ." Ken looked down at his falling-apart sneakers, his shaggy blond hair flopping over his forehead. "I couldn't have done it without your help. You know that, right?"

Maria fanned herself primly and batted her eyelashes. "Yes. I *am* an English genius."

Ken's eyes traveled back up to her face. "You are. Seriously. And I want to thank you somehow. How about we go to the movies tonight, on me?"

"Tonight?" Maria clicked her combination lock shut, her silver bangles jingling.

"Unless you have plans," Ken added quickly.

Plans? Right. Maria's social calendar wasn't exactly booked these days. "No," she told him. She smoothed out her long, floral-patterned skirt. "I don't. A movie would be fun."

Ken smiled. He looked as happy as a little kid who'd just been told he's going to Disneyland. "Really?"

Maria pushed a misbehaving curl of dark hair off her forehead. "Really."

"Cool!" Ken said. "Well, I gotta go catch Todd before class. I'll see you later?"

Maria nodded. "Later."

Ken took off, and Maria couldn't help smiling as

she watched him bolt down the hall, dodging crowds of people, his backpack flying behind him. It definitely felt good to be appreciated. She'd never seen anyone look so psyched to hang out with her before.

She shrugged, making her way toward math class. *I guess that's what friends are for,* she thought happily.

"Elizabeth! Please come in and take a seat!" Mr. Valasquez said, pushing himself out of his chair and smiling broadly.

There weren't many options in terms of seating in Mr. Valasquez's tiny yet bright office, so Elizabeth simply nodded and dropped down in the only available seat in the room—an old, black leather chair, complete with rips and tears and more than one gray bandage to show its age.

Mr. Valasquez returned to his chair, grinning at Elizabeth from across his cluttered desk. Elizabeth smiled weakly. Why was he greeting her as if she'd just won a prize on *Wheel of Fortune*?

"Don't worry," he went on, rolling up the sleeves of his plaid button-down shirt. "I'll write you a note for missing first period."

"Oh . . . okay." *Don't worry? Right.* Elizabeth was now sweating like mad. How long was she going to be in here? She was definitely going to need a dry shirt to change into if she was going to miss a whole class.

Mr. Valasquez was looking at her from behind his large, metal-frame glasses. No, *staring* at her. He had deep-set, very dark brown eyes that never wavered. Not knowing what else to do, Elizabeth just looked back at him, picking at the silver tape that covered most of the left arm of her chair. She shifted slightly, and her bare legs stuck to the seat.

She couldn't have been more uncomfortable if he'd trained a heat lamp on her.

"I bet you're wondering why you're here," Mr. Valasquez said finally.

Elizabeth's eyes darted back to his face. So he knew she didn't belong here! "Yes, actually, I am," she responded hopefully.

"Of course." He sat back in his chair, squinting at Elizabeth. "Well, Elizabeth, a number of teachers have expressed concern about you lately."

She bit her lip. *Expressed concern?*

"They say that you've been withdrawn," he continued, "and that you've been daydreaming a lot. And we have noted a sharp decline in your grades."

What? One C equaled a sharp decline? Elizabeth looked at the gray-industrial-carpeted floor, trying to absorb it all. For one brief period in her life she hadn't behaved like a model student, and now she was supposed to apologize or something?

Mr. Valasquez tapped a pencil on his desk. "Elizabeth," he went on. "You should know that there will be three progress reports going home."

Elizabeth's stomach dropped to her feet.

"But, uh, aren't those for people who are flunking?" she asked in a shaky voice.

Mr. Valasquez shook his head, giving her a small smile. "No, Elizabeth. They're for any student who makes a marked difference in their work."

She really wished he would stop saying her name. It only made it all the more real that she was here. And just what was he smiling about? This was *not* a smiling matter.

"Is there anything you'd like to talk about?" he asked gently.

Elizabeth blinked back at Mr. Valasquez as he took off his glasses and bit the end of the frames. What could she possibly want to talk to him about? After all, there was no way she could tell him what was really bothering her. What she was thinking about when all of her teachers complained that she was daydreaming.

Conner.

If she told Mr. Valasquez that whenever she sat down to work, she couldn't concentrate because all her thoughts were consumed by Conner—whether he was all right, if he'd ever forgive her, if they'd ever get back together . . . that *everything* seemed so unimportant compared to her feelings for him . . . Mr. Valasquez would just think she was a joke. A stupid, love-struck teenager. She couldn't bear to have anyone write off her feelings like that. Especially when they were so real. Too real.

Mr. Valasquez put his glasses back on. He began to stroke his beard. "Elizabeth, is everything all right at home?"

She looked down at her hands. "Everything's—" She glanced back up at Mr. Valasquez and cut herself off. His unreadable eyes were looking at her with such ferocious intensity. . . . She was about to say that everything was fine at home, but now she realized that he probably wouldn't let her leave unless she told him *something*. He would keep asking her questions or, even worse, just sit there and continue to stare at her until she finally let him in on her life.

She shifted in her seat again. Well, she wouldn't tell him about Conner. No way. But her home life of the last months had certainly been stressful enough to affect anyone's performance in school.

"Everything's what, Elizabeth?"

She pushed her hair behind her ears. "Well, actually . . . everything's kind of complicated."

Conner McDermott

My father was my idol.

Back in the days when I was just a skinny little kid with big hair, he was the one person I knew I could trust. Knew I could depend on.

After a long day of endless teasing by the neighborhood bullies, I would go over to my dad's house and spend the afternoon sitting on a paint can in his garage, watching my father as he played the guitar. I'd just sit there quietly in awe, my mouth slightly open, thinking that my dad was going to impart some great wisdom to me as he churned out his songs.

But he never did. He never taught me a thing. And then he left.

Actually, I think he did teach me something.

You can't depend on anyone but yourself.

Elizabeth Wakefield

I can't stand those 1980s John Hughes movies.

I know that everyone else loves them—Jessica rents them every chance she gets. And if <u>Sixteen Candles</u> is on TV, you can bet Jess is in for the night.

But I just think those movies are so stupid and superficial. That one, <u>The Breakfast Club</u>? It makes it seem like everyone in high school fits into this neat little category—you know, the popular princess, the stupid jock, the nerdy brain, the wrong-side-of-the-tracks rebel, the weird social outcast. I can't stand it when people stereotype like that. Why can't the princess also be the rebel? The jock also be the brain?

Wait a second. . . . Is that maybe the point at the end of the movie? That the princess _can_ be the rebel?

Hmmm. Maybe I should rent that one again.

CHAPTER 2
Suck It Up

"Of course the earthquake was horrible and scary," Elizabeth told Mr. Valasquez as she fidgeted with her necklace, "but the aftermath of it all was almost worse."

Mr. Valasquez leaned forward, resting his arms in the only available space on his messy desk. "How so?"

Elizabeth shifted in her seat. "Well, we lost our home, and that was pretty . . . traumatic."

He nodded, stroking his beard. "Of course."

Elizabeth let out a sigh. She was getting a headache just thinking about all of this. And she really didn't like it when Mr. Valasquez stroked his chin like that. He looked so pensive, his dark eyes all cloudy. It was impossible to guess what he was thinking.

"And then," she went on, crossing one sweaty leg over the other, "we moved in with my sister's best friend's—actually ex–best friend's—family. That was a nightmare."

She paused, waiting for Mr. Valasquez to say something. But he simply nodded for her to continue. Nodded and stroked his beard.

Was she supposed to just sit here and babble?

"They live in this huge mansion, which I guess some people would find luxurious, but I felt uncomfortable there," she explained. "It was like everyone was always watching my every move. And it just wasn't home." Elizabeth lifted her blond hair off her neck, trying to cool off. How could he stand this heat? "If you know what I mean."

Mr. Valasquez nodded again. "Sure."

"Anyway, I got in a fight with Lila—that's my sister's friend—and it got to the point that I couldn't live there anymore. So I moved in with another family."

Another nod. More beard stroking. "Okay . . . and how was that?"

Wonderful. Horrible. Nausea inducing. Elizabeth bit her lip as various adjectives flitted through her brain. "Uh, what do you mean?"

"Well . . . what happened while you were there?" Mr. Valasquez pressed.

I fell in love. I got kicked out by the person who I fell in love with. Am still in love with. She uncrossed her legs, then crossed them again, the backs of her thighs slippery against the now moist leather. "Not much, really," she mumbled.

Mr. Valasquez stared at her for a long moment. There he went, squinting at her again. *Does he know I'm lying?* Elizabeth wondered nervously. *It's probably written all over my face.* She averted her gaze, pretending to be really interested in the cheesy Every

Cloud Has a Silver Lining sign, set against a photograph of a sunset, on the wall next to her.

Mr. Valasquez cleared his throat. "But your parents were still living at the other house, correct?"

She looked back at him. "Uh, right."

Mr. Valasquez rested his chin in his hands. "And how was it to live apart from them?"

Elizabeth thought the question over for a minute. How *was* it? It was a lot of things. How could she possibly explain it to him—a virtual stranger? She couldn't even explain it to herself. "It was . . . hard, I guess. . . ."

"But?" Mr. Valasquez prompted.

"*But* . . . it was also kind of fun," Elizabeth admitted.

Mr. Valasquez's penetrating gaze finally seemed to soften. "Really? How so?"

"I don't know. I mean, I didn't see them very much, which was just as much my fault as it was theirs," she explained. "I did miss them, but I don't know. . . . I guess I didn't miss them as much as I thought I would. God, does that sound horrible?"

He shook his head, his expression almost reassuring. "Not at all."

Elizabeth moved to the edge of her seat. "It's just that I enjoyed having my independence and making my own decisions."

"I see." Mr. Valasquez nodded, but this time Elizabeth could tell that he understood. "And now? What's it like to be back home with them?"

"Kind of . . . weird." Elizabeth was surprised to hear the words come out of her mouth, but as she said them aloud, she realized that they were true. Things *were* weird. And it was a bit of a relief to admit it. "I mean, I'm happy to be back in my own house and more than happy to be living with my sister again. . . ."

"But?" Mr. Valasquez prompted again.

"*But . . .*" Elizabeth sank back in her seat. What *was* it that bothered her about being back home—aside from being away from Conner? "I guess it's a little hard adjusting to living with my parents. You know, having them tell me what to do now that I'm used to making my own decisions."

Mr. Valasquez took off his glasses again. He cleaned them with a tissue as he spoke. "That makes sense."

"It does?"

Mr. Valasquez nodded—the accepting nod—and for the first time that morning Elizabeth smiled for real. He understood. He wasn't blaming her for being annoyed with her parents. And, Elizabeth now realized, she had been feeling guilty about this for days without even recognizing it.

Huh. This meeting hadn't been *that* bad.

Mr. Valasquez glanced at his watch. "Elizabeth, I should let you go, but I would like you to come back and talk to me again next week."

"Next week?" Elizabeth's smile vanished. Why should she come back? She had just told him everything. Or, at least, everything she would ever admit to. "You know, I don't think that's necessary. I really feel much better, thanks."

Mr. Valasquez grinned. "I'd love to believe that I can make everything better in one class period, but I don't think that's the case. So, humor me. Next week—same time, same place?"

Do I have a choice? Elizabeth wondered, picking up her brown leather backpack as she stood. "Um, okay."

"I also wanted to let you know that I'll be calling your parents to let them know we've spoken," he said, putting his glasses back on.

Elizabeth's heart stopped. "Why?"

"Standard procedure," Mr. Valasquez said. "We think it's important that parents be informed."

I don't believe *this,* Elizabeth thought. She couldn't have spoken if she'd tried. Her parents were going to lose it.

"Lastly, I have a small assignment for you," he said. "Would you please go home tonight and write a list of your personal goals for the week? It's just for yourself. You don't need to show it to me. I think it might help to clear your head, get you more focused."

The bell rang. All Elizabeth wanted to do was get out of that hot, stuffy little office. "Okay, sure," she told him. "Bye."

And with that she bolted out of there—as fast as she possibly could.

*　　*　　*

Conner shook his head as Andy Marsden's flip-flop-clad foot slammed on the brakes in front of the house two doors down from Conner's. Andy shifted into reverse, hit the gas, and braked in front of Conner's driveway. *You'd think that after the hundredth time, Andy would get it right and not pass my house,* Conner said to himself. *But then, you'd be thinking wrong.*

"Well, later, man," Andy said, running a hand through his red hair and not even acknowledging his mistake.

"Later." Conner slapped hands with him, opened the passenger door, and jumped out. He was a little anxious to get home already. He wanted to make sure he put in some quality time with Megan after last night's fight.

"Oh, hey! McD.?" Andy called after him before he'd taken a step.

Conner turned around. "Yeah?"

Andy's blue eyes were bright. "Please inform your sister that stalking is inappropriate. We'll sign autographs, but that's where we draw the line."

"I'll let her know," Conner said with false sobriety.

Nodding, Andy drove off. Conner laughed to himself as he headed for his front door.

For the past couple of hours he and Andy had been chilling at their usual hangout, House of Java. Megan's two best friends, Wendy and Shira, were also there, and they had spent the better part of the

26

afternoon staring at Conner. Of course, every now and then they would look away and pretend to be engaged in conversation, but for the most part Conner had felt four eyes trained on his face, watching his every move. Finally, just as Conner and Andy were about to leave, the two girls got up the courage to say, "Tell Megan to call us."

Conner had a whole new respect for teen idols.

"Sandy?" he called as he opened the front door. Might as well relay her friends' ultraimportant message.

There was no response, but after a second Conner heard the unmistakable sound of Megan's laughter coming from the kitchen.

Conner headed for her but stopped short when he heard the sound of Gary's low voice. A sound that invariably made Conner cringe.

He froze in the doorway and saw that Megan and Gary were cooking together. *Cooking* together. No one in this family cooked. This was a pizza-three-nights-a-week household.

Conner rolled his eyes. The little slimy jerk probably thought that teaching Megan how to cook would score him major parental points.

And judging by the size of Megan's megawatt smile, it had. Gary was standing side by side with Megan at the kitchen counter, a roasting pan in front of them and a basting brush in Megan's slim hand. Gary was just a little taller than Megan but twice as wide, and his bald head was reflecting the sun. The only characteristic that indicated he was even remotely related to Megan was the reddish color of the tufts of hair above his ears and on the back of his head.

Gary patted Megan's shoulder, and she smiled. Conner felt like he was going to be sick. But there was nothing he could do. If he started up with Gary, Conner knew what would happen. Gary would turn everything around and blame it all on Conner. He'd spew his therapy crap as if it made any sense, then he'd try to exert his power over him. Conner knew where yelling at Gary got him. Absolutely nowhere. Not to mention how it would make him look to his sister.

He let out a short, frustrated breath. Last night's episode had showed him how Megan would react if he tried to get through to her. She was unreachable as long as her idiot father was around.

Conner narrowed his eyes as Gary crossed the kitchen and walked over to the refrigerator. He took in his ex-stepfather's atrocious red-and-white-striped button-down shirt that was too small for his body, his tacky brown moccasinlike shoes, and his navy blue socks. Megan would be so much better off if the jerk would just disappear.

Conner's neck muscles tightened with anger. There was nothing he could do about Gary trying to play father. Nothing at all. After his argument with Megan, it was clear she wouldn't listen to him on the subject. And her heart was going to be broken big time.

There was only one thing worse than the little faux *Father Knows Best* scene playing out in front of him.

It was the realization that he had no choice. If he couldn't talk to Megan, there was only one thing he could do.

He was going to have to suck it up and ask Elizabeth for help.

Personal Goals for the Week

- Study more. Get back to being an A student.
- Focus on the <u>oracle</u>. Start acting like an editor.
- Get Conner to talk to me.
- <u>Get my parents off my case.</u>

Elizabeth lay tummy down on her new mahogany sleigh bed before dinner, attempting to complete Mr. Valasquez's personal goals assignment. Why she was doing this instead of any of her other more pressing and more *important* schoolwork was a mystery to her. Except for maybe the fact that this required the least amount of concentration, something Elizabeth was running rather low on these days.

She sighed, putting down her pen as images of Conner floated through her brain. Conner dashing out of creative-writing class without so much as a look in her direction. Conner laughing with his friend Evan Plummer in the parking lot, his incredible green eyes lighting up with amusement. Conner glancing at her in the cafeteria and then—

"Liz?" her mom called from behind the closed door.

She sat up straight, quickly sticking her list of personal goals under the bed. An all-too-familiar feeling of panic came over Elizabeth. She'd been waiting for this moment ever since she'd heard her parents come in about an hour ago. It was going to be the Valasquez chat all over again. "Come in," she called.

Both Mr. and Mrs. Wakefield stepped into her room. *Together.* And they looked strange. Scared, almost.

"Hi, sweetie," Mrs. Wakefield said tentatively.

"Hi, guys." She looked from her mom to her dad and opted for the unconcerned approach. "Is everything all right?"

Mr. and Mrs. Wakefield shared a look. A parental look. One that said, *Should you tell her, or should I?*

Finally Mrs. Wakefield sat down next to Elizabeth. "Liz," she began, looking down at her lap and smoothing out her slim-cut gray suit pants. "We got a call from Mr. Valasquez today."

30

"I know," Elizabeth said.

"He told us that you met with him this morning." Mrs. Wakefield lifted her head, her blue-green eyes searching Elizabeth's face.

"Right," Elizabeth said. What were they expecting her to say?

"He explained about the progress reports," Mr. Wakefield added, dropping down into the plush burgundy chair next to Elizabeth's bed. He rested both of his hands flat on the armrests. "Liz . . . Mr. Valasquez seems to think that your living arrangements over the past few months have had a serious effect on you."

Elizabeth's eyes widened. She was in complete shock. Mr. Valasquez had never said he was going to *tell* her parents what they'd talked about. Weren't guidance counselors supposed to keep their conversations with students private? If she'd known he was going to tell her parents, she never would have—

"Why didn't you come talk to us?" Mrs. Wakefield asked, lightly touching Elizabeth's knee. Dumbfounded, Elizabeth stared down at her mother's graceful-looking, manicured hand.

"Don't you know that you can tell us anything?" her father said, his voice taking on a lawyerly tone.

Elizabeth suddenly felt suffocated. She looked from her mother to her father, her father to her mother—both of their eyes were wide with concern. Weren't there some things that she *could* keep to herself? Did she have to tell them *everything*?

"If we had only known this was happening . . . ," her mother said, clasping her hands in her lap.

Was that *disappointment* Elizabeth heard in her voice?

"Well . . . don't you think it's sort of obvious that living with strangers would have some sort of effect on me?" Elizabeth asked.

Mrs. Wakefield stood up, her face tightening. "Since when do you take that kind of tone with us?"

"*Mom*, I didn't mean—," Elizabeth began to explain, but her mom was already shaking her head.

"Don't forget that *you* were the one who begged to live somewhere else while the rest of us stayed at the Fowlers'," Mrs. Wakefield continued, wrapping her gray cardigan around her body.

Elizabeth let out a sigh. Could her mother *be* any more defensive? "I realize that, Mom, and I'm not blaming you guys, but—"

"*Blaming* us?" Mrs. Wakefield cut her off. She threw her hands up in the air.

Elizabeth stared back at her mother, stunned. Mrs. Wakefield's normally delicate, pretty features were now sharp and angry looking. And Elizabeth couldn't believe that she and her mother were actually having an argument. Where had this come from? "Mom, I never said—"

"Okay, okay, enough," her father broke in, holding up his hand like a cop trying to halt traffic.

32

Elizabeth's body filled with tension. She had a feeling she was never going to be able to complete a sentence in this house again.

Mr. Wakefield stood up and ran a hand through his thick brown hair. "Let's not fight," he said, walking over and sitting down next to Elizabeth. Suddenly Elizabeth just wanted to be as far away from her parents as possible. "The basic point is, we'd like to see you working harder in school."

Elizabeth nodded. She toyed with one of the little knots in her quilt. It's not like she hadn't worked hard her entire academic career. But okay, whatever, she could handle that. She swallowed. "Fine."

"And no more parties on school nights," he added.

Elizabeth froze. Was he saying what she thought he was saying? "Wait. Are you . . . *grounding* me?"

Her father shook his head. His dark blue eyes looked tired, the wrinkles in the corners especially prominent tonight. "Let's not call it that. Yet."

Yet? Were they expecting her to stage a rebellion sometime soon or something?

He stood up, shooting a glance at Elizabeth's mom. "And also we asked Mr. Valasquez to meet us all tomorrow after school."

A family trip to the guidance counselor? No way. Elizabeth scrunched her eyebrows together. "Tomorrow?"

"Yes," her mother said in a crisp, firm tone. "We'll meet you in his office. At three o'clock sharp."

Suddenly her mother was a drill sergeant.

Mr. Wakefield kissed her on her forehead, but Elizabeth barely registered it—she was too busy feeling like a guest star on an episode of *The Twilight Zone.* "Don't worry, sweetie," he said. "I know we'll work this all out."

Mrs. Wakefield nodded. A calmness now seemed to overtake her features, releasing the tension in her face. "We'll have dinner in a little while, all right?"

Elizabeth just nodded back.

Her parents walked out of her room, and Elizabeth grabbed one of her pillows, hugging it tight. She almost wanted to check around the room for hidden cameras. This had to be a practical joke.

Or a nightmare. She knew she hadn't been herself lately, but still. One bad semester and she had to go into counseling? Was everyone around her going crazy?

Or was she?

"That's one huge reason I'm glad my professional acting days are behind me," Maria said.

Ken took his eyes off the road to look over at her and almost lost control of the steering wheel. She was so beautiful. Especially when she was smiling like she was now, her huge brown eyes all sparkly against her milk-chocolate-colored skin, her dark curls flying around her face.

"Why's that?" Ken asked, refocusing on his driving before he ended up fender-to-tree.

"Because I don't have to act in pieces of crap like the movie we just saw," she said. Out of the corner of his eye Ken saw Maria pull a tiny tube of lip balm out of her little straw bag.

Ken smiled. "I didn't think it was *that* bad. . . ."

"Oh, Ken, please!" Maria used one long, slender finger to apply the lip balm, then smacked her lips. "The story was beyond stupid, the dialogue was a joke, and the—"

"Don't hold back," Ken teased as he stopped at a red light. "Give me your honest opinion."

Maria laughed, throwing the balm back into her bag. "You know I couldn't hold back even if I wanted to."

"Yeah, I do know," Ken said, pressing on the gas pedal as the traffic light turned green. Actually, that was the quality he liked most about Maria: the fact that she always said exactly what was on her mind. No holds barred.

"You really didn't think it was stupid?" Maria asked.

"No, I did," Ken responded. "But it was entertaining."

"Huh," Maria said. "I guess I was too offended to be entertained."

"Offended?" Ken made a left turn. "By what?"

"The way they portrayed teenagers, for one," Maria began. "All these movies make it seem like we're incapable of being with members of the opposite sex without wanting to jump them."

Ken felt a surge of blood rush to his cheeks. If

Maria knew some of the thoughts he'd had about *her* lately . . .

"And don't even get me started on the acting," Maria continued to rant. "I mean, that was most definitely offensive. Don't you think?"

"Uh, yeah," Ken agreed, pulling on the collar of his worn-in flannel shirt and grateful that she had moved away from the topic of sex. "The acting *was* bad."

"You know the lead?" Maria asked. "Allison Kelly Clark?"

Ken glanced at her as he came to another red light. She was looking ahead, so he focused on her profile. Specifically, he focused on her ear. She was wearing these small, purple-butterfly-shaped earrings, and they were just so . . . cool. "Yeah?" he said.

"Well, I used to act with her all the time. We were always up for the same parts. She was a total brat."

"Huh." Ken noticed that Maria had a beauty mark on her earlobe, just above her earring. Who knew that *ears* could be sexy?

"Ken?" Maria turned to look at him.

Ken's hormones went into overdrive. His heart raced. Was she having the same sort of thoughts he was? "Yeah?"

She signaled at the traffic light with her chin. "It's green."

Ken snapped out of it, and his cheeks flushed again. The car behind him honked. *You're* driving, *idiot, remember?* Ken shook his head, slamming on the gas a little too quickly. The car lurched forward. "Uh, sorry."

"That's okay," Maria told him breezily. She stretched her arms out in front of her. "Anyway, Allison was very snotty—and totally competitive. Would you believe that before one audition she actually hid the clothes I was going to wear so I wouldn't look prepared?"

Allison? Ken wondered, flustered. *Allison, Allison . . . Oh, right, the girl in the movie. Come on, Matthews. Get with it.* "Uh, you caught her?"

"No, it was just obvious," Maria told him. "Everyone knew she did it. And I got the part anyway."

Ken grinned at the competitive edge in Maria's voice. "Of course you did. She's a bad actress."

"The worst," Maria agreed, folding her arms across her chest.

"And ugly," Ken added. He turned down Maria's street.

Maria laughed. "Totally."

They reached Maria's house, and Ken put the car into park. He looked over at her once again, and suddenly, out of nowhere, his insides started to twist and turn.

Well, not out of *nowhere,* exactly. It was out of the fact that he really wanted to kiss her more than anything, and seeing that their date was coming to an end, he better make his move now or else—

"I had fun tonight, Ken," Maria said. She pulled her brown suede jacket on over her loose-fitting tank dress.

Uh-oh. That was a definite lead-up to "good night." Ken's palms began to sweat, and he found himself gripping at the sides of his seat cushion. "Even though the movie was so terrible?" he asked.

"Yeah," Maria said, hugging herself. She shrugged. "I have just as much fun trashing bad movies as seeing good ones."

Ken nodded. This was it. His perfect opportunity. If he could just lean in and grab her and kiss her . . . But Ken remained glued in his spot, unable to move an inch.

What if she pushed him away, disgusted? Or what if he had somehow turned into a terrible kisser in the past few weeks? Ken licked his lips, more scared than he'd been when he was about to be tackled by a two-hundred-pound Big Mesa linebacker. What if she *laughed* at him?

Maria tilted her head. "Well, I should head inside. Thanks again." She reached for the door handle, and Ken zeroed in on the wide, silver ring on her graceful ring finger. The sleek, thick band was embedded with a number of tiny red stones. Jewelry had never turned Ken on before—he'd never even *noticed* a girl's jewelry before. But then, everything about Maria turned him on.

"Good night," she said.

"Maria, wait—," Ken started. This was it. He was going to do it.

But when Maria turned around, her eyes questioning—almost shining—he lost his nerve.

"What?" she asked.

"It's just . . . uh, tomorrow's the Palisades Street Fair," he said, going with the first thing that popped into his brain. He wiped his sweaty hands on his jeans. "Ever been?"

She shook her head. "No."

"Well, I used to love it as a kid," he went on, feeling his earlobes burn up. "You wanna go?"

"A street fair?" Maria shrugged casually. "That sounds like fun. Yeah, sure, okay."

Ken smiled, relief flooding through him. So, he'd screwed up, but not totally. After all, Maria wouldn't agree to another date if she wasn't still interested, right? "Cool."

"All right," she said, buttoning up her jacket. "So, see you tomorrow?"

"See ya."

Maria stepped out of the car, and Ken watched her tall, slender frame disappear into her house.

Then Ken's shoulders slumped. He *had* made a quick save. But he couldn't let this happen tomorrow night. He couldn't wimp out. No way. But when he thought about getting up the nerve to kiss Maria, he froze, pure fear overcoming him.

Ken banged his head against the steering wheel. He had already decided that Maria's number-one quality was that she was the boldest person he knew.

He shook his head as he put the car into reverse.

Too bad he was such a coward.

Ken Matthews

<u>Five</u> <u>Reasons</u> <u>Why</u> <u>I</u> <u>Like</u> <u>Maria</u>
1. She's honest.
2. She's smart.
3. She's funny.
4. She's beautiful.
5. She's beautiful. (I think that one should count twice.)

Maria Slater

Five Reasons Why I Like Having a Close Guy Friend

1. I like getting a male perspective on things.

2. Guys are usually more direct and honest. They don't try to spare your feelings.

3. I feel like less of a dork spending a lot of time with him than I do when I'm constantly hanging out with my girlfriends. That might be pathetic, but it's true.

4. There's no chance we'll be interested in the same guy.

5. There's no chance we'll be interested in the same guy. (I think that one should count twice.)

CHAPTER 3

Things Are Getting Funky

There she was.

Kneeling by her locker as the post-first-period rush of students flew around her, Elizabeth slowly pulled out some books and stuffed them into her brown leather bag.

Conner swallowed. Why did she have to look so gorgeous? Why did he have to still feel so attracted to her head of silky blond hair, her tanned, bare shoulders—

Stop it, McDermott, he ordered himself. *Stop thinking about that, or you'll have to turn around right now and never say another word to her.*

Shaking his head, he walked over in her direction. He couldn't believe he was doing this. Couldn't believe he was actually asking *her* for help. Miss I Can Make Everything Better with a Smile. He hated the thought that she might actually think she was right.

This is for Megan, he reminded himself as he neared Elizabeth's crouched body. *She needs you to do this.* He stuck a hand in his front jeans pocket, looked down at Elizabeth, and opened his mouth before he could change his mind.

"Hey," he said.

For a second Elizabeth's body just froze like a statue. Then she lifted her head and glanced up at him, her face paling. Her shocked expression looked like someone had just told her that she got into Stanford. Either that or that her dog just died. In any case, she definitely looked like she was going to faint.

And, of course, she also looked totally beautiful.

Don't, Conner thought, his breath catching. He glanced up at the ceiling to avoid the intensity of her gaze. *Don't let her get to you.*

She slowly stood, pulled down on her heather gray tank top, and managed a soft, "Hi."

Great. She thinks this is some sort of reunion. "So," Conner said, wanting to get this over with as quickly as possible. "I take it you know about my mom and everything."

Elizabeth's eyes fell to the floor, then lifted to look back at Conner. Why did she have to look at him like that? Like she was trying to have a conversation with her eyes? Like she was inviting him in . . .

"Um, yeah," she responded. "Megan explained it to me."

Good old Megan. Tell Liz everything. "Right. Actually, Megan's what I wanted to talk to you about."

Elizabeth's eyebrows shot up. "Is she all right?"

"She's fine," Conner said, now making the mistake of staring directly back at Elizabeth's face. He could just kiss her . . . just reach out and pull her to him and—

He ran a hand through his scruffy hair, trying to shake off the attraction.

"She's fine for now. But she's going to be hurting in a few weeks when our mom gets back and her father is out the door."

"She doesn't know he's going to leave?" Elizabeth asked, looking right into Conner's eyes and making him regret coming to talk to her altogether.

He glanced down at his work boots. That's when he noticed Elizabeth's black sandals . . . and her deep-red-painted toenails. Not to mention her delicate-looking silver anklet. Since when did *Elizabeth* wear an anklet? God, the girl even managed to make feet a turn-on.

"No," he said, quickly darting his eyes away from her shoes and up to her . . . stomach. Her *bare* stomach, as the bottom of her tank top didn't quite meet the top of her black, wide-legged pants, thereby revealing a narrow strip of smooth skin. Conner wanted to touch that skin so badly; he wanted *her* so badly. . . .

Stop being insane, Conner ordered himself. *It's just hormones.* "Megan thinks Gary's going to stick around and marry our mother, and then we'll be a happy little family." He looked back at Elizabeth's face,

44

this time focusing on her chin to avoid the danger zone of her eyes. "Which is never going to happen."

"Are you sure? I mean—"

"Trust me," Conner stated. "It's not gonna happen."

She nodded, lifting a shaky hand to her hair. "And you—you tried to tell her this?"

"Yeah," he said. It took all of his mental energy to focus on *not* thinking about what it felt like to kiss those full lips. "But she won't listen to me. She thinks I'm biased because I hate the guy."

"Oh . . . ," Elizabeth said softly. Then she just looked at him, waiting.

God, she was going to make him say it. She would, wouldn't she? "So," he went on, "I'm asking you to talk to her."

In a flash Elizabeth's entire face—no, her entire body—visibly relaxed. And for a split second Conner thought he might have even seen a trace of a smile on her lips. *This is not about you, Liz,* he thought, annoyance shooting through him. *And it's definitely not about us. So don't look so damn pleased.*

"Of course, Conner," Elizabeth said. "I'd be happy to talk to her."

Conner nodded. This was what he had wanted, right? So now he should just thank her and get out of here. "Okay," he mumbled. "Good."

Elizabeth put her hands in her back pockets. She stared back at him for a long moment. Conner felt himself becoming drawn to her, pulled to her. . . . He focused on her sculpted cheekbones . . . on her silver, heart-shaped necklace hanging against her chest . . . on her lips.

Then she opened them to speak, and Conner turned around as quickly as possible. He'd done what he had to do. Now he had to get away. Fast.

"Conner—," he heard Elizabeth call after him, but he was already halfway down the hall.

And he was definitely not going to turn around. No way.

He couldn't trust himself not to grab her if he did.

Je sais anglais, mais je connais Marie-Ange.

A couple of minutes before the last-period bell rang, Maria hurried to scribble out her French homework. She'd been so exhausted after Ken had dropped her off last night that she'd fallen asleep before even starting it. Luckily this was so easy, she could do it practically without thinking.

"Hey, guys!" Elizabeth exclaimed, dropping down into the empty desk between Maria's and Jessica's.

Maria looked up from her paper and raised her eyebrows at her beaming friend. She had thought Elizabeth no longer had the mouth muscles necessary to form a smile.

But there she was—grinning for real.

"You look happy," Maria said.

"I do?" Elizabeth asked, taking her French books out of her bag and placing them on the desk in front of her.

"Liz, if your smile was any bigger, we wouldn't need a lightbulb in here," Jessica said, her perfectly plucked blond eyebrows scrunched together.

Elizabeth sat back in her chair, glancing from Maria to her sister, smile still intact. "I don't know," she said. "I guess I'm just in a good mood."

"Well, that's good to hear," Maria said. She'd thought her best friend was never going to come out of her Conner-induced funk.

"Wait. How can you possibly be in a good mood?" Jessica said, clearly surprised. "I thought after last night you'd be totally zombified."

Elizabeth shrugged. "Sorry to disappoint."

"What happened last night?" Maria asked.

"Nothing major," Elizabeth answered. "I got into a fight with my parents, that's all."

A fight? Maria dropped her pen midverb. She narrowed her eyes at Elizabeth. "You don't call that major? You *never* fight with your parents!"

Again Elizabeth simply shrugged. She began to doodle on the cover of her French book. Maria and Jessica shared a look of bewilderment.

"Well?" Maria pressed. "What was it about?"

Elizabeth let out a sigh. She gathered all her hair

up into a ponytail, wrapping a gray scrunchie around it. "It's stupid, really. Yesterday I got this pink slip and—"

"A pink slip?" Maria interjected. Now things were really getting funky. "You mean from the principal's office?"

"No, from Mars." Elizabeth laughed. She picked up her pen and continued with her doodling. "Of course from the principal's office."

Okay, something was seriously wrong here. "But Liz," Maria said, watching her carefully, "aren't those only for people who are flunking?"

Elizabeth shook her head. "That's what I thought, but no. It's really not a big deal. It was just a warning, you know, to make sure I stay on top of my work, keep focused, that sort of thing."

"Uh-huh," was all Maria could say. Elizabeth was always on top of her work. How could she dismiss this all so casually?

Maria cast a suspicious glance over at the cover of Elizabeth's *Le Français Aujourd'hui,* the target of all her doodling. The white spaces around the *n* and the *c* were completely filled in with blue ink, and the entire title was surrounded by little . . . *hearts?*

Maria sat back and chewed on her pen, taking in Elizabeth's twinkling eyes, her left leg that seemed to be bouncing on its own accord, her smile that wouldn't go away. . . . The girl was positively glowing. What the heck was going on?

"Anyway," Elizabeth went on, leaning forward in her seat. "I said I was in a good mood. Let's not ruin it by talking about this stuff." She smirked and looked at Maria out of the corner of her eye. "I called you last night, you know. Your mom said you were out with Ken."

The singsongy quality of Elizabeth's voice suddenly made Maria feel self-conscious. She took her pen out of her mouth and turned back to her homework. "Well, I was," she said, writing as fast as she could.

"You've been spending a lot of time with him lately," Elizabeth pointed out.

What did she mean by *that?* "And?" Maria responded.

"*So* . . . how was your date?"

Maria's mouth fell open. Then she laughed. "It was *not* a date! We just went to the movies. As friends. That's all."

"Who paid?" Jessica asked.

"Well . . . he did."

Elizabeth and Jessica nodded at each other knowingly.

"But that's only because he took me to the movies to thank me. For helping him with his English paper," Maria quickly added.

"Uh-huh," Jessica said, settling back in her chair and clasping her hands behind her neck. "Right."

Maria rolled her eyes, totally annoyed. Elizabeth

and Jessica both laughed. *God,* Maria thought, turning away from them and hurriedly trying to finish her work. *Do they have to act like twelve-year-olds?*

Ms. Dalton ran into class just as the second bell rang. "*Bonjour,* class!" she called out, dropping her ancient-looking brown briefcase on the desk at the front of the room.

"*Bonjour,* Madame Dalton," everyone responded in monotone voices.

Everyone except Maria. She was still trying to get past Elizabeth and Jessica's teasing. *Why can't guys and girls just be friends without everyone getting all suspicious?* she wondered. *I mean, they're acting like I'm keeping something from them. And I'm totally not.*

She sighed as Ms. Dalton gave an explanation in French as to why she was late.

Still, Maria thought, glancing over at Elizabeth's still giddy face, *no need to mention to her that I'm hanging out with Ken tonight.*

Again.

Elizabeth spotted Megan's red ponytail halfway down the hall.

She strode toward her, navigating her way through the after-school rush, unable to erase the perma-smile that had been on her face ever since Conner had approached her earlier today.

She knew that she shouldn't get too excited. Conner had asked for her help simply out of concern for his sister. It had nothing to do with how he felt about Elizabeth. But this did mean that he trusted her. That he was letting her in. Okay, so it was just a little bit, but still. It was enough to make her heart feel light.

"Hey, Megan," Elizabeth called as she neared her overall-clad friend.

Megan turned around, a dimple forming in her left cheek. "Liz! Hi! What's up?"

"Well," Elizabeth began, tossing her arm around Megan's shoulders, "you were just the person I was looking for."

"Really?" Megan asked. She allowed Elizabeth to steer her down the crowded hallway. "How come?"

"Because." Elizabeth pushed open the door to the stairwell. "We're going on a little road trip." She took her car keys out of her pants pocket and waved them in front of Megan as they walked down the stairs.

Megan stopped in place. "I'd love to hang out," she responded. "But aren't you forgetting about the *Oracle*?"

"Nah." Elizabeth pulled on Megan's skinny arm, leading her down the stairs again. "I think they can do without us for one day."

"If you say so." Megan shrugged, not sounding too sure. But she followed Elizabeth anyway, her ponytail and green backpack bouncing behind her.

"I say so," Elizabeth confirmed.

Then suddenly for some reason, she wasn't so

sure. Was there something she was forgetting? She paused, causing an extremely tall, blond-haired guy to nearly trip over her, but he kept his balance and continued on his way.

"Liz?" Megan called from the bottom of the stairs. "Is something wrong?"

Elizabeth shook her head. She was probably just feeling guilty about missing another *Oracle* meeting. Well, she'd make it up to Mr. Collins soon enough. "No," she called back. "I'm coming."

If it was anything important, you'd remember, Elizabeth told herself. *Don't worry about it.* And with that, she rushed down the stairs.

"So," Megan said when Elizabeth reached her. "Where are we going?"

"It's a surprise," Elizabeth told her, raising one eyebrow.

Megan laughed as they made their way through the bustling lobby. "You're insane, but I like it."

Twenty minutes later Elizabeth and Megan were sitting on red-cushioned stools at Casey's long, white counter, digging into old-school metal soda-fountain dishes, each filled with two enormous scoops of ice cream.

Elizabeth watched Megan glance around the old-fashioned-looking ice cream parlor. This place was always a comfort zone for Elizabeth. The entire room was decked out in red and white—all the stools and booth cushions were red, the tables and countertops white, and the floor, red-and-white tiled. The crisp white walls were lined with shelves holding shiny metal ice cream scoops, milk-shake mixers, and other relics from the 1950s. And as usual, Casey's was packed—mostly with kids from the junior high and middle school.

Elizabeth smiled to herself as Megan devoured a giant spoonful of her butter pecan. With her pony-tail high on top of her head, her freckle-covered nose, and her oversized denim overalls, Megan looked like a little kid herself.

"This place is pretty cool," Megan said, licking her spoon clean.

"Yeah," Elizabeth agreed. "It used to be my favorite hangout, actually." Elizabeth had decided that since she was feeling a little like her old self today, she might as well go someplace that her old self would approve of. Plus she thought that it might help to bring Megan to a new environment to get her to open up and talk. A place where she would just relax and have fun.

And judging by Megan's expression, Elizabeth had chosen the right place.

"I can see why." Megan gulped down another spoonful. "The ice cream is great."

"No kidding," Elizabeth responded. She watched a dreadlocked guy in a white uniform and red apron make a banana split behind the counter. "You know, it's probably a good thing that I don't come here that much anymore," she said, focusing on the split's maraschino-cherry-topped mound of whipped cream. "I could gain ten pounds just looking at all this ice cream."

"Please," Megan said. "As if you ever gain weight."

Elizabeth dug into her dish of coffee chip. "Believe it or not, it does happen."

Megan smiled. She wiped the corners of her mouth with her napkin. "I'm really glad we did this, Liz. . . . I miss you."

"I miss you too," Elizabeth said, tracing her spoon over her ice cream. She missed Megan, she missed Conner, and she missed living at their house and all the freedom it afforded her. And she still felt, more deeply than ever, that things could really become serious between her and Conner. If he just gave her a chance . . .

Enough, Elizabeth thought, forcing herself to snap out of it. *Stop it.* This outing was supposed to be about Megan. Sighing, she took another bite of ice cream. "So," she went on, swallowing. "How are things going at home?"

Megan began to swirl her remaining butter pecan into ice cream soup. "Pretty good, actually."

"Yeah?" Elizabeth said, searching Megan's green eyes. "You're getting along with your dad and everything?"

Megan nodded. "Totally. I mean, Conner's

Conner, of course. . . . But my dad's been great."

"Really?" Elizabeth asked, trying to sound non-chalant. "How so?"

Megan took another bite, apparently thinking this over. Then she put down her spoon. "It's just that there was this point when I thought my dad wasn't really ever going to be a part of my life. But lately he's totally been there for me. We do a lot of stuff together. It's cool to have him back."

"That's great," Elizabeth said, her heart twisting at Megan's words. Conner was right. His sister was definitely setting herself up for a huge disappointment.

"Yeah," Megan said. She smiled, fidgeting with her narrow, woven bracelet. "It really is. And I think I'm going to be seeing a lot more of him, you know?"

"That would be . . . nice," Elizabeth said. She stared at her sundae, hoping she wouldn't say anything to set Megan on edge. "But you know," she began, "it's hard to always know what people are thinking." She crumpled up a napkin and stared into Megan's eyes. "I mean, you said that your dad hasn't always been there, right?"

"Right. But now he's changed." Megan nodded slowly.

"That's the thing," Elizabeth said. "Parents are tricky sometimes. You can't *always* trust them. It's, like, you think they're one way, and then they surprise you with complete one-eighties."

Suddenly Elizabeth's words rang in her own ears. *Then they surprise you with complete one-eighties.*

She looked at her watch, and her stomach immediately dropped to the tiled floor. She couldn't believe she'd actually forgotten. . . .

Her parents! Valasquez!

Angel Desmond

To: tee@swiftnet.com
From: a.desmond@stanford.edu
Subject: I miss you

Hi, baby. How's life at home? Life here is already hectic. Training is starting to get really intense. We meet all the time. I guess they want to make sure that they don't have psychos advising the students. And I had my first computer-science class today. All I can say is, thank God I'm only auditing it. We already have a ridiculous amount of reading. If we have to read this much for a computer class, I don't even want to know what an English class is like.

I started my job at the campus store. Standard cashier kind of stuff. I get a discount, and I think you'll look mighty fine in a Stanford sweatshirt. You know, support your man and all that. :)

If you think you've encountered some strange characters in El Carro and Sweet Valley, just <u>wait</u> until college. There's this guy in my dorm who walks around all day in a ski mask. No joke.

Well, I gotta go to another peer-counseling training session. I hope you had a great day. Call me soon.

I love you.

Angel

TIA RAMIREZ

To: a.desmond@stanford.edu
From: tee@swiftnet.com
Subject: i miss you too.

angel—

hi, sweetie! your life does sound hectic but exciting, and i'm sure you can handle it all. do me a favor, though? stay away from that ski-mask guy. :)

all the new things going on in your life almost make my life seem boring. almost. but lately there has been enough going on to keep me rather oc-cupied. being cheerleading captain takes up more time than i would've thought. and my parents are on my case to start studying for the sats. as if i don't have enough schoolwork! i know, i know, it's nothing like college.

as usual, conner is a mess. and he's still not talking to liz, which appears to be making her a mess.

hey . . . come to think of it, maybe nothing has changed since you left.

except for the fact that you're not
here. and i miss you.
   i love you. talk to you soon.
                          tia

   p.s. i'd like my sweatshirt in gray,
thanks.

Spewing Parental Clichés

Jessica beamed, feeling as light and airy as a balloon as she, Tia Ramirez, and Jade Wu strolled through the parking lot over to Jade's car after cheerleading practice on Tuesday afternoon.

It had been an amazing day. Definitely the best day she'd had so far this year. So maybe that wasn't such an incredible feat, given the miserable nature of her first couple months of school, but still.

To begin with, for some unknown reason Elizabeth had actually been chipper. Suspiciously chipper, considering the fact that she'd gotten a pink slip the day before. But Jessica wasn't about to dwell on that. It was enough for now that her sister had managed a smile.

What had really put this particular afternoon over the top was that she'd seen Will exactly six times over the course of the day. And each time he'd done or said something extremely cute. Like pulled her into a supply closet to steal a quick kiss. Or given her a weedlike flower (it's the thought that counts) that he'd picked off the school grounds. Or simply

61

smiled at her, his gorgeous gray-blue eyes crinkling in the corners . . .

"Hey, Mary Sunshine." Tia nudged Jessica with her elbow as they walked. "You might want to turn down that grin a notch. Melissa's Will radar is bound to go off any second."

Jessica shrugged, pulling down on her gray cotton athletic shorts. "That's her problem, not mine." Jessica did feel bad for Melissa. The girl obviously had serious problems, and the last thing Jessica wanted to do was rub Melissa's face in Jessica and Will's budding romance. But she also refused to feel guilty anymore. It wasn't her fault that Melissa needed help.

"Whatever," Jade said. She took her purple elastic out of her ponytail, causing her long, stick-straight dark hair to fall down her back. "I'd still watch out if I were you."

As if on cue, Melissa's two sidekicks from hell, Cherie Reese and Gina Cho, sauntered up to Jessica, Tia, and Jade at that very moment.

"Hey, Tia, Jade," Gina said, flipping her sleek black hair behind her shoulder. "Wait up."

Jessica stopped along with her friends, crossing her arms over her chest. Of course they weren't even going to acknowledge her presence. As if she cared.

"What's up, guys?" Tia asked, the tone of impatience obvious in her voice.

Cherie tilted her head, her red hair falling across

half of her pale-skinned, narrow face. She gave Tia and Jade a saccharine-sweet smile, pointedly ignoring Jessica. Jessica just sighed. When were these girls going to graduate from the fourth grade?

"I wanted to tell you about my party tomorrow night," Cherie said. "My parents are in Hawaii. It's gonna be a rager."

"Oh. Cool," Tia responded, her voice anything but enthusiastic. Her brown eyes looked bored.

"Yeah," Jade added. She picked an invisible piece of lint off her purple T-shirt. "Cool."

Jessica couldn't resist a smile at Gina and Cherie's surprised reactions to Tia and Jade's lackluster responses. What had they expected them to do, perform back flips out of excitement? Even when they were being blatantly rude to Jessica?

"You guys will be there, won't you?" Gina asked, her dark eyes almost suspicious.

"Probably. I guess," Jade told them.

Tia shrugged. "I never miss a party," she said, her tone still neutral.

"Well, this is going to be the party of the year," Cherie said, then quickly gave Jessica a look as if to say, *And you're going to miss it—so there!* Jessica almost expected Cherie to stick out her tongue. *So immature.*

Sighing, Jade glanced down at her pink Cinderella watch. "Guys, I gotta get to work," she said.

Cherie nodded. "Yeah. We've got some things to

buy for tomorrow night." After one last taunting look at Jessica, Cherie and Gina turned away, heading for the other end of the parking lot.

Tia shook her head and Jade rolled her eyes as they walked with Jessica toward Jade's black Nissan. "God. I can't believe them," Jade muttered.

"You think they take bitch pills in the morning?" Tia teased, gathering her wavy dark brown hair up into a messy bun.

"No," Jessica said. "I think it comes naturally."

Tia and Jade both laughed, but then Tia looked at Jessica, her eyes sympathetic. "Sorry, Jess."

"Please," Jessica said. She opened the small front compartment of her black leather backpack as they walked, searching for a pack of gum. "They don't get to me anymore. I can't believe they ever did. They're so lame." She finally found the cinnamon gum she was looking for and pulled it out, offering both Tia and Jade a piece.

Jade took a stick and unwrapped it, popping it into her mouth.

"Agreed," Tia said, taking a piece as well. Then she smiled. "But you know what's even lamer?"

"What?" Jessica asked, unwrapping a stick for herself.

"I'll probably go to Cherie's party anyway," Tia joked.

Jade laughed. "Me too."

Jessica grinned as they neared Jade's car. "Of course. A party's a party."

"Right," Tia said. Then she grabbed Jessica's arm,

squeezing it. "Hey, you know what? You should still come. What are they gonna do, kick you out?"

Jessica stopped in place and raised her eyebrows. "Who are we talking about here?"

Tia bit her lip, smiling, her trademark dimple forming at the corner of her mouth. "Oh, yeah. I guess you're right."

Jessica shook her head. It felt so good to not care. Finally. "Don't feel bad, Tee," she said as Jade unlocked her car's driver's-side door. "I wouldn't go to that party if you paid me. Seriously."

Tia and Jessica walked around to the other side of the car. "Okay . . . but you and Liz and I are still on for tonight, aren't we?" Tia asked, opening the passenger door. She popped the front seat forward. "You haven't forgotten about our let's-keep-Tia-company-since-Angel's-gone plans, have you?"

Jessica laughed, climbing into the back. "You've only reminded me, like, ten times."

"Huh." Tia put the passenger seat back and slid onto it. "I guess it would be hard to forget, then."

"Right," Jessica responded. But as she settled into her seat, she couldn't help thinking that at the rate Elizabeth had been going, *she* just might forget.

Please don't be mad. Please don't be mad. Elizabeth's hands were so sweaty against the Jeep's steering wheel that she was afraid she might lose her grip altogether.

She had just dropped Megan off at her house and was now racing to get home. It was too late to try to meet her parents at school. Elizabeth glanced down at the speedometer, and her heart skipped a beat. The last thing she needed was to get a speeding ticket. Should she slow down? Elizabeth bit her lip. *No. I have to get home as soon as possible.*

But when she finally reached her tree-lined driveway, Elizabeth suddenly had the urge to be anywhere but there. They were going to be *so* mad. She drove slowly up to the two-car garage, her pulse racing and her hands shaking.

Once she put the car in park, Elizabeth sat inside it for a moment, taking a deep breath and trying to collect herself. She wiped her sweaty hands on the soft, upholstered seat cushion. Maybe they wouldn't be *that* mad. Elizabeth had never been late to anything in her life before. She never got into trouble. They couldn't get that angry if this was her first time, right?

Wrong. Elizabeth had her answer as soon as she walked inside and saw her father's face. He was sitting at the kitchen table, his dark blue eyes small and tense looking, his mouth formed into a tight, thin line. And that tiny vein above his left eye was pulsing.

He was most definitely mad. Or worried. Or both.

"Liz! Where have you been? Are you all right?" he demanded, jumping up once he saw her.

"I'm fine, Dad." Elizabeth took a tentative step

toward him. *Stay calm,* she told herself. *You can explain. He'll understand.* "I'm really sorry. I forgot about the appointment and then—"

"You *forgot?*" he repeated, his voice getting louder and his face turning as red as a tomato. *So much for understanding.* "How? We just told you about it yesterday!"

Elizabeth nodded, shuddering at her father's tone. He'd never yelled at her like that before. She wasn't sure if he'd ever yelled at *anybody* like that before.

Maybe I should make up something, she thought, feeling desperate. *Maybe I should tell him that there was some emergency at the* Oracle *and—*

Elizabeth shook her head. Livid or not, this was her *father.* She couldn't lie to him. "I know," she began quietly. "And I didn't *really* forget about it. I just lost track of time."

"This is so unlike you." Mr. Wakefield gripped the back of one of the tan kitchen chairs, leaning his weight down on it.

Elizabeth's shoulders collapsed with a rush of relief. He was going to let her off the hook. He realized that this was a onetime event. An honest mistake. "I know, Dad," she said, stepping closer to him. "I don't know how I forgot, but I—"

"'I don't know' is not going to cut it," Mr. Wakefield interrupted angrily, standing up straight. He turned his gold wedding band around and around on his finger. "Do you know that your mother is so worried, she's driving around the neighborhood looking for you right now?"

Elizabeth's shoulders tensed up again. "What?" Wasn't that a little extreme?

"Yes." Mr. Wakefield turned his back on Elizabeth, leaning on the Formica counter and staring into nowhere. "Not to mention the fact that you made a fool out of us in front of Mr. Valasquez."

Elizabeth's mouth involuntarily dropped open. Did it really matter what the school guidance counselor thought of him? "Dad, I said I'm sorry. I—"

"Well, sorry isn't enough." Her father turned around, his face still completely red. "This is it. You're grounded. For real this time."

Elizabeth sat down at the kitchen table, feeling dizzy. Had she just entered an alternate universe? Was this really *her* father standing before her, spewing parental clichés as if they were going out of style?

Then the reality of his words sank in. He was *grounding* her. "But Dad," she said, looking up at him. "I have plans with Tia and Jessica tonight."

"Not anymore, you don't," her father told her, continuing on with his bad-sitcom-father lines. "You are not to leave this house for two weeks except to go to school. No friends, no phone, no nothing."

Elizabeth stared back at him for a moment in disbelief, then focused on the geometric design etched into the border of the wooden kitchen table, her eyes watering.

She had always been the good girl. She had never

understood why kids would purposely disobey their parents. But here she had gone and made one mistake and her dad had completely freaked out. In a more than unreasonable way.

Suddenly Elizabeth had a whole new understanding for the need to rebel.

Conner shook his head as he walked downstairs. He was about to have his second irritating conversation in two days . . . all for Megan's sake. *She better thank me one day*, he thought.

When Megan had come home late that afternoon, she mentioned that she had been hanging out with Elizabeth. So Elizabeth had tried to talk to her. Whether she got through to his sister at all remained to be seen.

And now he was about to attempt some damage control with Gary. Let the jerk know that moving a random woman into this house would be the worst decision ever—as if it wasn't painfully obvious to anybody with half a brain.

Conner reached the bottom of the stairs and closed his eyes for a moment. The thing that was going to particularly suck about this conversation was that Conner was going to have to remain calm and controlled around his ex-stepfather, no matter how idiotic Gary was. Because one thing was certain: Gary would refuse to listen to Conner if he lost his temper.

Conner took a deep breath and headed for the living room. Sure enough, there was Gary, his stocky little body sunk into the overstuffed beige armchair as he read some stupid psychology journal. Conner's skin instantly started crawling.

Ignore it, Conner told himself. *Just get through this.* He cleared his throat.

Gary looked up from his magazine. "Hello, Conner. You missed dinner again."

"Yeah." Conner took another step into the room. "I grabbed some pizza."

Gary's lips formed into a mocking smile. "You must like pizza a lot. That's all you ever eat."

Conner tried to ignore the rising tension in his muscles. "Yeah." He sat down on the brown couch next to Gary's chair. "There's something that needs to be said."

Gary closed his journal and placed it on the glass coffee table. "About what?"

Conner looked him right in the eyes. "Your girlfriend."

Gary sat up straight, his thick red eyebrows knitting together. "How did you—"

"I overheard you," Conner explained. And before Gary could get angry, he quickly added, "I came to Mom's room to talk to you, and you were on the phone with her. I heard you talking about moving her in here."

"Well." Gary crossed one leg over the other. "Sounds like you *accidentally* overheard quite a bit."

"No," Conner responded. "I didn't." He stood and walked over to the window, unable to stay seated and control his anger at the same time for a moment longer. He looked back at his ex-stepfather. "Gary, she can't move in here. It will kill Megan."

"Hmmm." Gary nodded. He reached into his striped oxford shirt's front pocket, pulled out a box of cigarettes, and proceeded to light one. As if his teeth weren't nicotine stained enough already. What a great role model for Megan.

But as Gary took a long drag from his cigarette, he actually seemed to be mulling Conner's words over. Bizarre.

Conner walked back over to the couch and leaned against the armrest. "Think about it," he said. "I know she's your girlfriend, but the last thing any of us needs right now is a stranger wandering around the house, getting involved in our business."

Gary nodded again, taking another drag. "Uh-huh."

Conner stared at him and waited, his patience wearing thin as the smell of smoke surrounded him. It seemed like the jerk was never going to respond.

Finally Conner stood up straight, turning his back on him. He couldn't take this anymore. He refused to sit there and—

"I won't move Alicia in," Gary announced.

Conner froze. "What?"

"I said I won't move Alicia—my girlfriend—in," Gary repeated.

No way. It had worked. The guy had actually listened to him for once. Conner turned to face him. "Gary—"

"*If*," he interjected, pointing one finger in the air. "If you start to behave yourself."

Conner's hand clenched into a tense fist inside his pocket. "*Behave myself*"? What was this, kindergarten?

"That's right." Gary stood, finally putting his cigarette out in the shell-shaped ashtray on the coffee table. He ran a hand over his head. "I'd like you to set a good example for Megan. Show some respect in this house."

Conner's body was as tight as a pulled rubber band. But he only had to hold it in a minute longer. Then he could go upstairs and punch a hole in his wall. "What do you mean?" he asked through clenched teeth.

"Well, for starters, show up for dinner tomorrow night," Gary began. "*On time*. And look respectable. Then we'll talk some more about Alicia."

There was fire raging inside Conner's body, but on the outside he was as cool as a sheet of ice. "Yeah," he said. "Okay."

Conner thought he saw a flicker of surprise cross Gary's pale, pasty face, but he didn't stick around to take a second look.

Not a chance. Not when there was a wall upstairs with his fist's name on it.

melissa fox

Most people underestimate the importance of details.

Take Jessica Wakefield, for example. People like her only concentrate on the big picture. So she has Will—for now. But I'm not worried. Not at all. Why's that? Because big-picture types like Jessica are careless. They overlook the tiny details, and those are always the most important.

For instance, Jessica might have Will—for now—but she doesn't have loyal friends. Lila is a prime example. Didn't take long for her to side with me. And Cherie, being the good, <u>loyal</u> friend that she is, made a point of not inviting Jessica to her party tomorrow night. meanwhile I have no doubt that all of Jessica's friends will show up, not caring that Jessica isn't welcome. And guess who else will be there?

Will. Oh, and me, of course.

So yeah, when you look at the big picture, Jessica has everything. But when you break it down, she has nothing.

And Will is bound to realize that before long.

The Rebel Thing

5

If I don't get it this time, I swear this game is rigged, Ken thought as he squinted, aiming the small ball in his right hand at the perfectly stacked white wooden pins before him.

In about seven minutes he had spent fourteen dollars at this booth, idiotically trying *and failing* to knock ten of the twelve pins down with the ball. *I'm an athlete,* he'd figured when they'd first stepped up to the booth. How hard could it be?

Impossible, it turned out.

"Maybe your arm is just tired from practice or something," Maria said.

"Yeah, right," Ken muttered. "Maybe if they ever let me throw the ball." He'd spent the afternoon riding the bench once again, watching Will Simmons get the workout of a lifetime. Coach had finally let him take a few snaps at the end of practice, but he'd barely had time to warm up before he had to hit the showers. Now he was topping off that perfect experience by repeatedly humiliating himself in front of Maria.

75

So why was he being such a sucker? Why was he practically throwing his money away?

"You're gonna get it this time," Maria told him, patting him on the back. "I feel it."

Right, Ken thought, grinning. *That's why.* It might be sappy, but Ken really wanted to win Maria a stuffed animal. He thought that despite the cornball element, the gesture would still be kind of romantic.

He glanced at Maria. She was dressed very casually tonight in jean shorts and a light green sweater, but she looked more gorgeous than ever. Ken could hardly keep his eyes off her long, toned legs.

"You really think this is even possible?" Ken asked.

She nodded, giving him a look of mock seriousness. "Oh, yes. Definitely."

Ken looked back at the pins. He pulled back his arm, aimed, and released the ball.

All twelve pins went down in an instant.

Ken's jaw dropped open. "You did it!" Maria exclaimed, grabbing onto his arm. "You did it!"

"A prize goes to the gentleman in the blue baseball cap!" the bald man behind the booth called out.

"What did I win?" Ken asked.

"You have your choice of anything on this shelf." The guy took a long, wooden stick and pointed at the third shelf up, which was crammed with games, stuffed animals, and bright, fuzzy, ambiguous objects.

Ken turned to Maria. "Which one?"

Maria shook her head. "You pick," she said. "It's your prize."

"I know," Ken told her. "But I want you to have it."

Her dark eyes opened wide. "You do?" Ken nodded. She smiled, her entire face lighting up. "That's so sweet!"

"Excuse me?" the man behind the booth interjected, looking from Ken to Maria. "We need to get on with this."

Maria laughed, putting her hand over her mouth. Ken watched her as she scanned the prize shelf, her eyes twinkling. He didn't need a reward for knocking down the pins. Seeing the psyched expression on Maria's face was prize enough.

"I'll take that one," Maria said finally, pointing up at a soft-looking pink teddy bear with a purple bow tie.

The man knocked the bear down with his stick and handed it to Maria. She beamed as she looked down at it. *Score two points for me,* Ken thought happily, stuffing his hands in the pockets of his khaki pants.

"Ever notice that the stuffed animals at carnivals are always weird colors?" Maria asked as they walked away from the booth.

Ken stared at the bear and frowned. "Do you want to exchange it?" he asked.

"Oh, no!" Maria exclaimed, holding the bear close to her chest. "I like the fact that he's pink. He's . . . offbeat."

"Oh, okay," Ken said. He swallowed, glancing down at Maria's graceful, slender hands as he and Maria continued to walk around the fair. She was holding the bear in her left hand, leaving her right one free. Should he try to hold it? he wondered, his pulse racing. If he could just—

Then Maria wrapped both arms around the bear. Ken's heart plummeted. He'd missed his chance.

Maria held the stuffed animal in front of her face. "I think I'll name him Pinkie," she declared.

"Pinkie," Ken said with a smile. "That works."

"I want one! I want one!" All of a sudden an adorable little girl with red pigtails and chocolate smudges on her face was standing before them, pointing up at Maria's bear. A thirty-something-looking woman—most likely the girl's mother—was immediately by her side.

"We'll find you one, Anna," the woman assured her. She gave Ken and Maria a desperate look. "Where did you get that?"

"Actually, he won it," Maria explained, motioning to Ken. "But just barely. These games are all impossible."

"But I want a bear, Mommy!" Anna called out, stamping her foot. "I want one too!"

The girl's mother looked exasperated. She crouched down beside her daughter. "I said we'll find you one, sweetie. But we might have to go to a store to get it."

Anna shook her head, her pigtails flying from

side to side. "I want one like that! I want a pink one!"

Anna's mother raised her hand to her forehead. Clearly she'd had a long day with her daughter.

"Here," Maria said, thrusting the stuffed animal at the girl. "You can have this one."

Ken's jaw dropped. Wasn't Maria missing something here? He had *won* that bear specifically for *her*. How could she just give it away like that?

Anna was now hugging the bear tightly, her eyes closed.

"You really didn't have to do that," the girl's mother said to Maria. She looked down at her daughter. "And I'd insist on giving it back, but I'm afraid of the scene that might cause."

Maria waved her off. "It's no big deal," she said, making Ken feel about as tall as Anna. Maria knelt down and gave the girl a serious look. "Just remember, his name is Pinkie."

"Pinkie," the girl repeated, then kissed the bear's face.

"Thanks again," Anna's mother said, clasping Anna's shoulders. "Well, have fun."

Maria nodded. "You too."

Once the girl and her mother had walked away, Maria turned to Ken and bit her lip. "I hope you don't mind that I gave it to her."

Ken kicked at the ground. "Mind? Oh, no, I don't mind."

"Good," Maria said. "I just felt like such an idiot standing there—a seventeen-year-old clutching a stuffed animal that a five-year-old wants more than anything. You know?"

Ken swallowed, nodding.

Yeah, he knew what being an idiot felt like. After all, he was the one who'd thought that winning Maria a stuffed animal would be romantic.

Jessica had found her recipe for the perfect night.

One House of Java mochaccino with extra whipped cream and one Will Simmons. Those two things were all she needed to make all the fighting that was going on at home seem miles away. That and the fact that Jeremy was off tonight, so she had no reason to be looking over her shoulder.

"I'm sure Liz'll be fine," Will said as he poured almost an entire container of sugar into his coffee. "She's just doing the rebel thing."

Jessica placed her green-and-purple-patterned coffee mug down on the table. "You think?" she said, tracing the mug's rim with her finger. Somehow the words *Liz* and *rebel* didn't seem to go together.

"Yeah. I think." Will leaned forward and swiped at the top of Jessica's lip with his finger. Jessica's heart flip-flopped at his touch. "You had some whipped cream," he explained, his eyes crinkling in the corners as he smiled.

Jessica gazed back at him, her pulse racing at a crazy rate. She licked the remaining whipped cream off her top lip. God. Could he possibly be any cuter?

"Hey! I hope you don't mind that I brought a last-minute Liz replacement," Tia announced, breaking the supercharged moment and pointing at Andy as she dropped down in the empty seat next to Jessica. "But then again, it looks like you brought one too," she said, gesturing at Will.

Jessica nodded, hugging her pink cardigan closer to her body. "The more the merrier."

Andy pulled out the chair across from Tia. "I'm so glad I'm only your backup," he commented, sitting down. "I'll remember that next time, Tee."

Tia rolled her eyes. "Quit the dramatics, Andy. As if I don't always ask you to come with me wherever I go."

"Yeah, when Angel's not around," Andy quipped. "I am so very honored."

Will turned to Andy and placed a firm grip on his shoulder. "*I'm* glad you came, man," he teased in a deep, mock-serious voice.

Jessica laughed. Nope. It wasn't possible. Will couldn't be any cuter than he already was. "Me too," she told Andy.

"Well, thanks," Andy replied as he shrugged off his black jacket. "It's nice to know I'm appreciated."

"So, what's this about Liz getting grounded?" Tia asked. "She called me to apologize for not coming, but she didn't want to get into it. . . . What's going on?"

Jessica sighed. "Wish I knew. For once I have no idea what she's thinking."

Tia sat back in her seat. "Well, I think *I* know

who's been occupying her brain space," she said, crossing her arms over her chest. "A certain six-foot, dark-haired, guitar-playing someone, whose butt I'm gonna kick the next time I see him."

"No." Jessica shook her head, twirling a blond strand of hair around her finger. "Conner might be part of it, but he can't be all. Trust me. I know my sister, and she is acting *weird.*"

"I don't know," Andy said, shifting in his seat. "Considering how straightlaced you all say she's been for the past seventeen years, I think it would be *weird* if she didn't break out just a little."

"Yeah." Will nodded. He balanced his chair on its two back legs, holding on to the edge of the small, square table. "That's what I said."

Jessica shrugged. "So maybe you guys are right." She picked up a stray napkin and played with it, crumpling it up into a ball. "Anyway. At least she'll have to stay home and keep me company while you're all at Cherie's party tomorrow night."

Will dropped his seat forward on its front legs. "Who said I was going to Cherie's?"

Jessica blinked. "*Everyone's* going to Cherie's."

"Yeah," Andy said, helping himself to some of Will's coffee. "It's gonna be huge."

Will leaned forward across the table. He stared into Jessica's eyes. "But *you're* not going, right?"

Jessica shook her head. She wrapped both hands around her coffee mug. "No, but I—"

"Right. So I'm not going," Will told her. "Why would I want to go anywhere that you're not welcome?"

Jessica's mouth fell open. There was no possible way she could have found her tongue at that moment.

Out of the corner of her eye Jessica saw Tia and Andy exchange an amused look, but she ignored them, keeping her focus on Will. On his thick, blond hair that curled just a little bit toward the nape of his neck; on his casual, easygoing half smile . . .

"You sure?" she asked him. "I mean, I don't want you to miss out or anything."

Will let out a short, amused breath. "Jessica. The only way I'd be missing out would be if I didn't see you."

Wow, Jessica thought, taking Will's hand.

"All right, guys, enough," Andy said with a groan. "There are two other people here at the table with you."

"Hey, yeah," Tia put in. She looked from Will to Jessica, raising one dark eyebrow. "And this was supposed to be about keeping *me* company, not about making me miss Angel more with your little love fest."

Jessica giggled. She actually *giggled.* God, she was so dorkily giddy! But she didn't care. This was what being with Will did to her. And she loved it. "Sorry," she said, looking at Tia but still holding Will's hand.

"Yeah, sorry about that, Tee," Will added.

"That's all right," Tia joked, pushing her dark, wavy hair behind her shoulders. "Just don't let it happen again, or you won't be invited back."

Will squeezed Jessica's hand, and she looked back at him, losing herself in his eyes. It didn't matter what Tia said. As far as Jessica was concerned, Will would be invited back again and again.

Maria stared out of the passenger window of Ken's car. The star-filled night sky looked like an infinite deep blue blanket, spread out over the valleys below.

She wrapped a curl of hair around her finger. "It's such a clear night," she murmured.

"Yeah."

Maria turned and glanced at Ken. His dulled eyes were completely trained on the road in front of him, his mouth in an almost frown. He was never a big conversationalist, but for the past hour or so, he'd been practically mute. And he seemed so morose. *Maybe he's thinking about Olivia,* Maria thought, her heart constricting out of sadness for him.

"Ken? Are you all right?" she asked softly.

"Yeah," he responded, not taking his eyes off the road. "Just tired."

Maria looked back out the window. Ken seemed to be a lost cause tonight. But he'd been so happy earlier. They'd had so much fun together—more fun than she'd had in a long time. . . . She only hoped he snapped out of it soon. He'd come so far in these past few weeks, it would be horrible if he fell into a total regression or something.

Soon she heard the sound of the tires rolling over her gravel driveway. Ken drove right up to her front door, pulling to a stop.

Maria looked down at her lap. The car was thick with silence.

She sighed. *Better just leave him be and call it a night,* she thought, turning to take off her seat belt.

But at that moment Ken turned as well and opened his mouth as if to speak. Then he quickly snapped it shut.

"What?" Maria asked. "What were you going to say?"

A glint of hopefulness appeared in his blue eyes. "Maria, I—," he began, then shook his head, breaking off. "Never mind."

"Are you sure?" Maria pressed, moving to the edge of her seat and closer to him. "I'm up for talking."

Ken shook his head again. "No," he said. "That's all right."

He looked so unhappy . . . and so confused—like a little boy. In a sudden swell of tenderness for him, Maria reached over and gave him a peck on his surprisingly soft cheek. "Feel better," she whispered.

In an instant his face lit up with a smile.

Maria grinned, thrilled by the effect her small gesture had on him.

"Thanks," he said, looking back at her with a sheepish expression.

"No problem," she responded. Which was the

truth. If all Ken needed was some caring, someone to look out for him . . . well, Maria was more than happy to be the one to do that. It made her feel special—like she was capable of doing something nobody else could. "Good night, Ken."

"Good night, Maria," he said, his voice as energetic as it had been earlier that evening.

Maria opened the car door and stepped out, refreshed by the feeling of the cool night air hitting her bare legs.

And by the fact that she was apparently able to lift Ken's entire mood.

Jeremy Aames

I thought I was pretty mature the other day when I asked Jessica if she was going out with Will. It wasn't easy, and it most definitely sucked when she told me that yes, she _was_ seeing the guy. But I didn't have a choice. I have to move on. And I don't have the time to be hung up on her forever.

That's why I feel like such a wimp. I stopped by House of Java tonight to check the work schedule, and I turned right around when I saw that Jessica was there . . . with _Will._ Yep, that's right, I bolted right out of the place. I know what you're thinking. _Coward._ _Wuss._ And you're right. But what could I do? It actually hurt to see her . . . with him.

Anyway. That's it. From now on, I'm going to pretend that Jessica Wakefield never existed. Erase her from my mind. That shouldn't be too hard, considering that between football, my job, and watching my sisters, I barely have a minute to think anyway.

I do have one small problem, though.

I'm going to have to rearrange my entire HOJ schedule so that I never have a shift with her again.

"How did Mom act to you this morning?" Jessica asked Elizabeth as Jessica drove their Jeep out of the Wakefields' driveway on Wednesday.

"I really don't want to talk about it," Elizabeth muttered.

Oo-kay. Jessica pulled on her black cat-eye sunglasses to combat the morning glare of sunshine. *So much for helping Liz talk through her problems.* She flipped on the radio as she made a right turn, running through the stations until she found a sufficiently upbeat song to cheer her sister up.

"Will snuck the sweetest note in my backpack yesterday," Jessica began, hoping to turn her sister's attention to other things.

"That's nice." Elizabeth gave her a small, obviously forced smile.

"I know! I found it last night when I pulled out my math notebook. Isn't that cute?"

"Yeah."

Jessica glanced back over at her twin. Elizabeth was staring down at her lap, her eyes watery.

Jessica braked at a stop sign. *Okay, scrap that tactic.* Maybe she'd be better off talking about the crappy aspects of her life.

"Do you know what Gina and Cherie did to me yesterday after cheerleading?" Jessica asked, pressing on the gas.

Elizabeth glanced up, her eyes now filled with concern. "No. What?"

Aha! Jessica thought. *I got her!* "Well, I was with Tia and Jade and they came up to us, but they totally ignored me, of course. Then they invited Tia and Jade to Cherie's party tonight just so they could talk about it in front of me and *not* invite me. Do you believe that?"

"Cherie's having a party tonight?" Elizabeth asked.

Jessica's forehead creased. "Yes. That's what I just said."

Elizabeth dropped her head back against her seat. "That's great," she mumbled. "Cherie's having a party, and I get to sit home and watch some more bad television."

Jessica nearly crashed the car into the black Honda ahead of them. Since when did Elizabeth make such a big deal about parties? Jessica was the one who usually cared. And *Jessica* was the one who was socially banned from the event.

"Come on, Liz. You can't really mind that you're missing that lame party," Jessica chided lightly.

"Besides, I'll be home with you. We can hang out."

"Right," Elizabeth muttered, picking at the door lock.

Jessica's patience was beginning to run out. Her grip tightened on the steering wheel. "Don't sound so excited," she responded sarcastically.

"Oh, I'm sorry, Jess," Elizabeth said, dropping her hands in her lap and sounding like herself for the first time that morning. "I'm just so annoyed with Mom and Dad."

"I know." Jessica drove into the almost filled school parking lot. Luckily she spotted an empty space immediately. "But please, don't get all upset that you're not going to Cherie's. It's not worth it." She shifted gears into park and cut the engine. "I'm sure you won't miss a thing. I bet no one's going anyway."

"Yeah," Elizabeth said, opening the car door and smiling slightly. "You're probably right."

Jessica hopped out of the Jeep, relieved. At least she had made a little bit of progress with her sister. She straightened out her black sundress. All she had to do was keep being upbeat with her and maybe—

"Hey, Wakefields!" Jake Collins called, passing them on his way to the school entrance. "I'll see you guys at Cherie's party, right?"

Jessica cringed inwardly as she saw Elizabeth's face fall.

Jessica rolled her eyes. *Great. So much for making progress.*

* * *

Was Mr. Quigley one of the teachers who complained about me? Elizabeth wondered as she listened to her creative-writing teacher give a lecture about points of view. She sank deep into her seat, biting on her pencil. Was there now not one adult she could trust?

Mr. Quigley didn't usually spend the class lecturing. Most of the time he led the class like a workshop, picking some people to share their pieces and asking the others to critique it. But Elizabeth was glad for the change of pace. She wouldn't be able to concentrate on anyone else's writing enough to comment intelligently on it, and if he asked her to read aloud—forget about it. At the moment Elizabeth was so depressed, she wasn't even sure if she was capable of speech.

As she sat there and numbly focused on Mr. Quigley's graying ponytail as he wrote the words *Narrator—reliable or unreliable?* on the chalkboard, she realized that she hadn't processed a single word he'd said today. She was too busy thinking about the fact that for the next couple of weeks she was going to have no social life. None whatsoever.

God, I'm wallowing. I hate it when people wallow. Elizabeth sat up straight, pushing her hair behind her ears. *Wonderful. Now I'm angry at myself for feeling sorry for myself . . . which only makes me feel more sorry for myself.*

Ugh. Elizabeth's head pounded. Was she ever going to snap out of this?

Suddenly a folded-up piece of lined notebook paper landed on her desk. Her heart thudded in response. And once she unfolded the note and glimpsed the jagged handwriting, her entire body was met with an enormous rush of emotion.

Conner.

Elizabeth took a deep breath to steady her heartbeat as she focused on his words:

Liz:

I know you spoke to Megan. Thanks.

Conner

It definitely wasn't much, but what could she expect? Conner was never one to be verbose. And just the fact that he was speaking to her again, actually going out of his way to *thank* her, was enough. The silent treatment was over. Maybe.

She smiled. So all the adults around her suddenly seemed to think that she was some sort of dangerous delinquent, she officially had no life, and she was still feeling sick to her stomach from all the Golden Grahams she'd consumed last night.

But Conner didn't hate her. Now, *that* was something to be happy about.

*   *   *

Maria paused from her note taking to stretch out her hand. She was just about to lift up her pen again when Madhavi Reddy, the girl who sat in the desk to the left of hers, passed her a note.

Maria looked at the piece of paper and smiled. Ken. It had to be. He was the only person who wrote notes to her in history class. She glanced at Mr. Ford to make sure he wasn't looking in her direction, then unfolded the note.

Hey, Maria:
    Want to grab dinner before
Cherie's tonight?

                    Ken

Dinner? Tonight? For some reason, the sight of those words in Ken's masculine, messy handwriting suddenly made Maria freeze up. After all, if they had dinner, this would make it the third night in a row that they'd gone out together. It had been easy to deny that anything was going on between them when Elizabeth and Jessica had teased her about it the other day, but, well . . . what *was* going on?

Let's review, Maria thought, staring down at the note. The movies. That was just a way of paying her back for helping him out . . . wasn't it? Maria swallowed. All right, so then they went to that fair together . . . and he won her a stuffed animal. Maria lifted her dark curls off her neck, suddenly feeling warm. And then Ken looked like he might burst with happiness when she gave him a small kiss on his cheek last night. *Uh-oh.*

But is it really *uh-oh?* Maria wondered all of a sudden. Would it be a bad thing if Ken was interested in her? Maybe she could like him too. Maybe they'd make a good couple.

Without realizing it, she started to scribble little hearts and stars in the margins of her notebook, then quickly crossed them out, her cheeks feeling hot.

Maria looked over her left shoulder to steal a glance at Ken, to try to read what he was thinking, but his expression betrayed nothing. He was focused on Mr. Ford, engrossed in his lecture. Or at least pretending to be engrossed.

She turned back around, feeling stupid. She and Ken were just friends. Buddies. Amigos. She had simply let Elizabeth and Jessica put crazy ideas in her head.

Maria rolled her eyes at her own silliness. Really. Just because she and Ken spent a lot of time together didn't mean that anything was developing between them. She and Elizabeth could hang out every night of the week—that's what friends did. It was the same thing with Ken. Except, of course, that he was a guy.

She glanced back down at his note. Besides, he'd asked her to "grab" dinner. Nothing romantic there. Maria shook her head. Ken was an honest guy. If he wanted to go out on a real date, he'd ask her.

She tore a small piece of paper out of her spiral notebook and scribbled on it, determined to put all of these outrageous thoughts out of her mind. She was about to fold the note when she read over her words and frowned.

Ken:

I'd love to have dinner before the party! Want to pick me up at eight?

Maria

She'd "love" to get dinner? Didn't that sound just a tad too enthusiastic? And asking him to pick her up at eight . . . wasn't that making it sound like a date? She didn't want to send the wrong message or anything.

Maria crumpled up the piece of paper and ripped off another one. She quickly jotted down another response.

Dinner would be fine. Let's talk later.

She scratched her head. Was that a little too *un*-enthusiastic? She didn't want to hurt his feelings or anything. And he might even catch on that she was purposely trying to sound cool because she was worried he liked her or something. Then he would confront her about it and promise that he only liked her as a friend. She cringed. That would be *so* embarrassing. And she'd had her fill of humiliation from the opposite sex lately.

Sighing, she ripped off yet another piece of paper. She thought for a moment, then began to write.

> *Ken:*
>
> *I'd like that. Where do you want to go? I've been craving Italian. . . .*
>
> *Maria*

Maria quickly folded the note over, wrote *Ken* on it, and passed it over to Madhavi.

She'd done it. Looking up at Mr. Ford, she picked up her pen again. There was just one problem. She was going to have to copy Ken's notes from today since she had spent the better part of the class trying to compose a three-sentence, appropriately platonic response to him.

She shook her head. Was this what all girls and guys who were friends went through? Because Maria was starting to remember the benefits of having close *female* friends . . .

*   *   *

"So. Who's gonna rage at Cherie's tonight?" Andy asked, sitting down across from Elizabeth in the noisy, crowded cafeteria.

Elizabeth groaned inwardly as she pushed her faux mashed potatoes around on her plate. Any excitement she'd felt from getting Conner's note in creative writing had completely vanished. First of all, Conner was now eating at the other end of the long, white table, next to his friend Evan. He hadn't so much as looked at Elizabeth the entire day. Clearly he was glad that she'd spoken to Megan, but that was it. He still didn't want to have anything to do with her. Not at all.

And to top it all off, everyone was talking about Cherie's. *Everyone.* Elizabeth could have sworn that even the kitchen staff were planning on attending the bash.

"I'm in," Conner said, lifting his chin at Andy.

Elizabeth glanced up, and her heart tumbled to the food-stained floor. Conner was going to Cherie's, and Elizabeth was going to be home playing Trivial Pursuit with Jessica.

She continued to smash her potatoes, trying desperately to drown out the party buzz that crowded her ears. *This whole grounding thing is beyond ridiculous,* she thought, her grip tightening around her fork. *I'm late for one meeting, and Mom and Dad can't trust me?*

She dropped the fork, pushing her tray away

from her. The sight of her food suddenly made her nauseous. *I should just blow Mom and Dad off and go anyway,* she thought, feeling like she was going to explode.

Tia touched her arm. "What about you, Liz?" she asked. "You up for tonight?"

Elizabeth turned to look at her friend's smiling face, and for a second she almost said yes. *Almost.* But then she shook her head. As angry as she was, she just couldn't disobey her parents. It was impossible. Doing the right thing was practically a force of habit for her at this point. "I can't," she whispered. "I'm grounded."

Tia winced. "Ooh, that's right. Sorry."

"It's okay," Elizabeth managed.

After all, it was all Elizabeth's fault. She sighed, sneaking a glance in Conner's direction. *She* was the one who got herself trapped in this role of the good girl.

Ken Matthews

<u>Checklist</u> <u>for</u> <u>tonight</u>

- Make reservations at Enzo's.
- Clean the car—vacuum the inside.
- Find an unwrinkled shirt. If I can't find one, buy one.
- Brush my hair.
- Go to the ATM. Pray I have enough money in my account to cover dinner. If not, ask Dad for money.
- Kiss Maria.

I can't believe I'm doing this, Conner thought as he tucked his clean, white, button-down shirt into his khaki pants. He never bothered to brush his hair for a girl, and now he was primping for *Gary,* of all people?

"Megan," Conner muttered. "It's for Megan, not Gary."

He glanced over at his digital clock radio—6:28. Almost show time. Shaking his head, he walked out of his bedroom.

Megan was already in the kitchen, setting the table while Gary cooked. She did a double take when she noticed Conner standing in the hallway. "Mac! What's with the clean-cut look?"

Gary turned from the stove and looked Conner up and down, his red, bushy eyebrows lifting, his face especially pale. Apparently he was surprised by Conner's attire as well.

Conner shrugged, trying to ignore the tensing of his neck muscles. "No reason," he said, strolling into the kitchen. He picked a slice of cucumber out of the large wooden salad bowl on the counter and popped it into his mouth.

Megan froze, forks and knives in hand. "Are you . . . are you having dinner with us?" she asked.

Conner shot a look at Gary, who quickly glanced away. "Yeah," he told Megan. "I am."

Megan's eyes lit up. "Really?" she asked, dropping the silverware on the table. "That's great!" She quickly ran to the drawer by the sink and pulled out another knife and fork, hurrying to put them on the table. But then, as she reached up to take another plate out of the cupboard, she hesitated for a moment. "Are you sure you're feeling all right?" she teased, placing one hand on her hip.

"Yeah," Conner told her, managing to form a tiny smile. *Aside from being nauseous from this whole scene,* he thought, glaring at Gary's back.

"Cool." Still beaming, Megan continued with her table setting.

Conner sighed. At least Megan was happy. He peered into Gary's pot of tomato sauce. "Smells good," he forced himself to say.

"Oh . . . thanks," Gary responded tentatively. He didn't bother to make eye contact with Conner.

Whatever, Conner thought, walking away. It was useless to try to talk to the jerk. Why bother? All he had to do was make it through this meal.

"Oh, Megan, we're going to need one more setting," Gary said, taking off the apron.

Megan's forehead creased into little intersecting lines. "But I already added one more for Conner."

Gary kissed her cheek, and Conner shuddered at the sight. Man, this was *not* going to be easy. "I know, sweetie," Gary told her. "But tonight I've invited a surprise guest."

Conner froze. *He wouldn't.*

"A surprise guest?" Megan repeated, obviously confused.

"Yep." Gary grinned, his beady eyes dancing. "And I can't wait for you to meet—" The doorbell rang. "Ah! That's her!"

Conner's stomach turned over as Gary hurried out of the room. His limbs felt paralyzed, the reality of what was about to happen sinking in with great force. *He couldn't,* Conner thought. *Not after we—*

"Here she is!" Gary announced. He then proceeded to usher in an extremely thin woman with brown, curly hair, half of which was up in a barrette. She wore a long, black dress and was a good two inches taller than Gary. Not to mention the fact that her freckled, young-looking face indicated that she couldn't be that much older than Conner.

He did. Conner clenched his teeth.

"Megan, Conner," Gary went on. "I'd like you to meet Alicia . . . my fiancée."

Conner's entire body stiffened with anger. He looked at Megan. Any semblance of color had drained from her face.

"Your fiancée?" she repeated weakly. "But you never mentioned . . ." Her voice trailed off, and her green eyes darkened.

"I know." Gary walked over to her, placing a pudgy hand on her shoulder. "I was waiting for the right moment, honey."

Sure, Conner thought bitterly. *And this moment is just ideal.* For a shrink, this guy really knew nothing about people.

"I've heard so much about you." Alicia beamed, her small, dark eyes opening wide. She strolled over to join Gary and Megan and held out a frail-looking hand. "It's wonderful to finally meet you."

Conner watched as Megan slowly, shakily shook Alicia's hand. "Yeah," Megan whispered. "You too."

Alicia turned around and smiled at Conner. "It's a pleasure to meet you as well."

All Conner could do was nod. The damage was already done. Megan was obviously trying very hard to keep it together. Conner was proud of her composure. And he knew that if he opened his mouth and blew up—which he was on the verge of doing—his sister would collapse in a second.

"Well." Gary clapped. "Why don't we all sit down? Alicia, take the seat without the setting. I'll grab you a plate."

Conner watched Alicia as she dropped into a chair, all smiles. Who did this woman think she was?

Conner slowly walked over to the table and sat

down next to Megan. She was putting on an okay facade, but Conner knew she could break at any moment.

Megan looked down at her plate and pulled her napkin onto her lap. "So, um, are you from Seattle?" she asked Alicia, her eyes cast downward.

"Yes." Alicia nodded. "Well, actually, I'm originally from Denver. But I've been living in Seattle for a long time now."

Yeah, sure, Conner thought. *All of your teenage years, right?*

Gary placed a plate and silverware in front of Alicia and sat down next to her, clasping her long, slender hand in his short, stubby one. Conner noticed that Megan flinched at the gesture. "And for the next few weeks, at least, Alicia's going to be a resident of California," Gary added.

"Oh." Megan looked at Alicia. "Are you staying nearby?"

Alicia opened her mouth and then closed it, looking at Gary uncertainly. Gary winked at her. "*Very* nearby," he told Megan. "That's part of why she's here tonight. Alicia's going to be staying with me. She's moving in."

"Moving in?" Conner saw the flash of hurt and anger cross his sister's face. And then she snapped. Her green eyes narrowed into tiny slits. "What?" she exclaimed, her cheeks flushing pink. "What are you talking about? She can't stay here!"

"Come on, honey." Gary motioned with his hands

for her to take it down a notch. "Why don't you calm down, and we'll all talk about this like adults?"

"What do you mean?" Megan yelled, ignoring him and standing up. "I don't even know her!"

"And that's why she's here," Gary said slowly, as if he were talking to a young child. "So that you *get* to know her. Now, you need to take a deep breath and stop being so hysterical."

"She doesn't *need* to do anything," Conner snapped, the fury spewing out of him. He'd been quiet for long enough, and just look where it had taken them. "You're the one who strolled into her life and forced some random woman on her."

Gary looked at Conner, his blue eyes cold and distant. "Stay out of this. This is between me and my daughter."

Megan began to cry. "No, it's not," she said, the tears spilling down her now blotchy cheeks. "Because I don't want to have anything to do with you!" In a flash she ran out of the room and up the stairs before Gary could say anything more.

Conner glared at Gary for a second, but his ex-stepfather simply stared back calmly. *Of course. Why should he care that he's destroyed his daughter?* Conner swore under his breath, then took off to go after his sister.

When he got upstairs, Megan's door was closed, but he could hear her crying on the other side. He tapped on the door. "Sandy? It's me."

No response. Just the sound of choked sobs.

"Come on, Sandy," he said softly. "Let me in."

"I want to be alone for a while," she finally responded in a faraway voice. "Leave me alone. Please?"

Conner sighed. He could do that. She needed her space, and he had to give it to her. He'd already let her down enough as it was. "Yeah. Let me know if you need anything, all right?"

No response again. Conner stood there for a minute longer, then he turned and barreled back down the stairs. He could let Megan be alone for a little while, but there was one person in this house who he was definitely not going to leave alone. Not by a long shot.

"What the hell do you think you're doing?" Conner demanded when he found Gary still at the kitchen table with Alicia a moment later.

"Don't use that language with me," Gary warned. "Remember, we talked about respect?"

"Screw respect!" Conner exploded. "You went back on everything we 'talked' about anyway!"

"Now, listen. I didn't go back on anything," Gary insisted, standing up and placing his hands on Alicia's bony shoulders.

"You told me—"

"I *told* you that if you came to dinner, we'd discuss Alicia. Which is exactly what we were doing."

Conner let out a short breath. "We both know what you said. You can lie all you want, but we both know you said you weren't moving her in here."

Gary walked a step closer to Conner. "Let me remind you of something. I am the parent here. I make the decisions. And if I want my fiancée to live here with me, then she will. End of discussion."

Conner shook his head. "Funny," he muttered. "You don't act like a parent." Then he pushed past Gary and stalked away.

He couldn't stand to look at the guy for another second.

Maria hugged herself as she and Ken walked up the stone pathway leading to Enzo's, an Italian restaurant in Big Mesa. It was a chilly, windy night, and she was trying to warm herself up. She was also trying to calm herself down. She still wasn't quite over the mini freak-out she'd had over Ken in history class today. *Relax,* she thought, rubbing her goose-bump-covered arms with a vengeance. *You and Ken are just hanging out.*

Ken opened the thick glass door and motioned for Maria to go ahead as he held it open. Maria smiled, but all of her senses instantly panicked to date-alert mode. So now Ken was acting like a *gentleman?*

Maria quickly walked ahead, blushing a bit. It was nice that Ken was being so polite and all, but his chivalrous behavior felt strange, to say the least. Not to mention the way he was dressed. He'd forgone his usual old denim jacket for a crisp, new blue sweater. *And* he was wearing a pair of brown suede bucks rather than his beat-up sneakers. A tight knot began to form in Maria's stomach. It was getting harder and harder to ignore the suspicions she'd had earlier today.

Then Maria walked inside and felt *very* strange. The restaurant was beautiful. It was painted a deep burgundy color and was darkly lit, filled with intimate tables and candles. *Lots* of candles. In a word, the room was romantic. In three, romantic and sexy. Very sexy. Maria bit her lip.

"Cool place, isn't it?" Ken asked from behind her.

Cool? Well, Ken *was* a guy. Maybe he didn't realize how romantic the restaurant actually was. "Yes," Maria answered, still rubbing her arms. "It's . . . cool."

Suddenly a tall, scrawny woman dressed all in black materialized before them. "Do you have a reservation?" the woman asked them.

"Yeah." Ken stepped forward. "Matthews. For two."

The woman consulted her book at the hostess stand, then smiled coolly. "Right this way," she told them, grabbing two menus.

Maria looked at Ken, and he motioned for her to follow the hostess first. Maria grinned back at him, but on the inside she was freaking out. Did this cozy dinner mean something? Was he interested in her? Or was Ken really that clueless and didn't realize what messages he was sending?

When they reached their small, corner table by the fireplace, Maria quickly sat down in the first chair the hostess pulled out, not wanting to wonder whether Ken was going to carry on his Prince Charming role and offer the seat to her.

The hostess handed her a menu, and she glanced around the room at the elaborate flower bouquets, the dripping white and burgundy candles, the twenty-something couple to the left who were kissing as if there were no tomorrow . . . and then back at Ken.

Maria suddenly felt queasy. Why was he gazing at her like . . . *that?*

Uh-oh. She swallowed. *Major uh-oh.*

Conner lay on his bed, staring blankly at his guitar across the room, surrounded by a thick, empty silence.

It was a welcome silence, though. A silence that meant that Megan was no longer crying pathetically in her room. And that Gary was no longer laughing it up with Alicia downstairs, carrying on as if his daughter's heart wasn't breaking in the very same house.

Conner sat up, his anger at his ex-stepfather once more threatening to overwhelm him. If the guy wasn't Megan's father, Conner would have knocked him out long ago. He picked up his pillow and hurled it across the room, narrowly missing his guitar. Maybe he still would.

Conner had hoped that this one time he would be wrong about his ex-stepfather. That the guy would manage *not* to disappoint Megan. How could he have been so stupid?

He knew better.

Conner walked out of his room and knocked on his sister's door. "Megan?" he called.

No answer. But Conner did hear the muted sounds of the television coming from inside her room. *She must have passed out,* he figured. *Cried herself to sleep.*

Conner slowly creaked open the door and stepped inside. The room was dark, illuminated only by the flickers of light coming from the television set. He walked lightly so as not to wake her and reached over to the red power button on the TV. He was just about to hit it when he glanced over at his sister's bed.

It was still made. And empty. Megan wasn't there.

"What the—?" Conner ran to switch on the light. There was a yellow piece of paper on Megan's fluffed-up lacy pillow. He grabbed it, quickly reading the note.

I'm sorry. I can't live here with them.

Conner's heart began to race. What did that mean? Where the hell had she gone? And *when?*

His palms sweating, Conner glanced over at the window. They were on the second floor. There was no way Megan could have gotten out that way.

She must have just walked out the front door, Conner realized, his stomach twisting and turning. How could he not hear her? How could he let this happen? She could be anywhere . . . doing any*thing*.

Conner began to panic as a million possibilities ran through his brain. His eyes fell on Megan's ragged brown teddy bear with only one eye that she'd had since she was two. A sinking realization made his heart feel heavy.

She could've been gone for hours.

Elizabeth sat on her blue-and-white-striped window cushion, hugging her legs and staring out into the darkening evening sky. She was bored out of her mind, and she'd had enough TV to last her a lifetime. After watching an hour or two of talk shows this afternoon, she'd remembered why she wasn't a big television fan to begin with.

Jessica had wanted to hang out after dinner, obviously wanting to cheer Elizabeth up. It was thoughtful of her, and Elizabeth felt horrible for not wanting to, but the truth was, it hurt Elizabeth to be around her sister. She was so perky . . . so happy. Everything that Elizabeth wasn't.

Besides, Elizabeth didn't feel like doing anything at all. Not talking. Not reading. Not playing a game.

Nothing. Nope, she just wanted to sit here and sulk.

And think about Conner.

She stretched out her legs as she watched her neighbors, the Amadors, get into their minivan across the street. She knew that it was a waste of time to occupy her mind with thoughts of Conner. He'd made it clear that he still didn't want anything to do with her.

But then again, she had all the time in the world to waste. And it was useless to try to put him out of her mind. Plus, she had to admit, she still carried the glimmer of hope that he would want her back one day. Every time she thought about the pain she'd seen in his eyes, about how much he must be hurting, about how he'd actually thanked her for talking to Megan . . .

Megan! Elizabeth bolted up.

Was that actually Megan racing down the sidewalk on her bike in front of Elizabeth's house? Elizabeth knelt and pressed her face to the glass, trying to get a better look. It was definitely her, and she was headed right for Elizabeth's front door.

Elizabeth immediately stood up and hurried out of her room, quietly but quickly rushing down the stairs as fast as possible, her heart beating in her ears. Taking a deep breath, she swung open the front door before Megan could ring the doorbell and disturb her parents.

"Liz!" Megan exclaimed.

"Shhh!" Elizabeth glanced inside to see if her parents had heard. There was no movement from the study or their room. She turned back to Megan. "I'm not allowed to have friends over," she whispered.

"Oh." Megan's eyes instantly filled with tears. "I should go, then."

Megan was about to step away when Elizabeth saw how horrible she looked. Her eyes were red and puffy, her skin was all blotchy, and she looked like she was shivering in her army green sweatshirt and jean shorts. "No, don't go," Elizabeth whispered, grabbing onto her arm. "Megan . . . what's wrong?"

Megan glanced at the ground. "Everything!" She looked back up at Elizabeth, and her nose turned bright red.

Elizabeth searched her face. "Is it your dad?" she asked gently.

"Uh-huh." Megan nodded, tears starting to fall down her face, her long hair sticking to her wet cheeks. "You were so right. I just had to get out of my house. I've been riding and riding, but I have nowhere to go. . . . So I came here." Her breath was coming out in short, shallow gasps.

Elizabeth pulled her into a hug. Her heart stung as Megan sobbed uncontrollably into her shoulder. The poor kid. As if she hadn't gone through enough already. "All right, it's okay," Elizabeth murmured. "Let's go upstairs."

"No," Megan protested, pulling away. She wiped her eyes with the palm of her shaky hand. "I don't want to get you in trouble."

"Trust me. This is more important," Elizabeth insisted, staring into Megan's heartbreakingly sad face. "Just try to be quiet on the way up, okay?"

Megan nodded slightly. "Okay."

Once they were in the safety of Elizabeth's room, Elizabeth sat Megan down on her bed. "Close your eyes for a second and relax," Elizabeth told her.

Megan followed her instructions as Elizabeth walked over to her night table and grabbed a box of tissues. Then she plopped down next to Megan. "So you've been riding around for a long time?" she asked.

"Yeah," Megan responded, taking a tissue from Elizabeth. She blew her nose. "I just couldn't go back home."

"And you told Conner where you were going?" Elizabeth asked.

Megan picked up one of Elizabeth's pillows and hugged it close to her body. "No."

Elizabeth bit her lip. She was sure Conner would be wondering where his sister was. She stood, grabbing her cordless phone off the desk. "You should call him, then. You know, just to let him know you're all right," she said, handing the phone to Megan.

But Megan just stared down at the pillow. "I can't talk to him, Liz," she said, new tears springing to her eyes. "Not yet."

"Not even for a minute?" Elizabeth persisted gently. "He's probably worried about you."

"I know." Megan's voice cracked as she began to cry again. "And I *will* call him. In a little while. I just need some time first. . . . What if my dad answers?" Her watery eyes pleaded with Elizabeth, and her hands tightly grasped the pillow. "Please?"

Elizabeth regarded her friend for a moment. Part of her wanted to insist that she call. Conner was a protective older brother, and if he'd realized that Megan was gone, there was no doubt that he was going crazy trying to find her.

But Megan looked so desperate, so sad. It couldn't hurt to wait a few minutes to let Megan talk things through first, could it?

"Okay," Elizabeth said, placing the phone behind them on the bed. "Why don't you tell me what happened?"

Andy Marsden

To: a.desmond@stanford.edu
From: marsden1@swiftnet.com
Subject: Yo

Angel, what's up? How's life in northern Cali? Not too much is new with me, but I promised to keep you in the loop while you're at school. And as usual, I seem to be the only person who knows everything that's going on around SVH. So, here goes.

Situation #1: Okay, anyone can tell that Ken and Maria totally want each other. And I mean anyone. But Maria insists that she and Ken are only friends, while it's obvious that Ken already thinks they're on their way to being a couple. So one of them is definitely in for a surprise.

Situation #2: Conner's having a really tough time lately. A lot of his problems are out of his control, which you know he doesn't like. Still, there is one thing or, I should say, one <u>person</u> that he does have control over. If he would just be a man and admit his feelings for her, he'd be a much happier guy. Which brings me to . . .

Situation #3: Elizabeth. I thought
Jessica was exaggerating the other day
when she said Liz wasn't acting like
herself, but now I understand why
Jessica's worried. Her parents grounded
Liz, which means she can't go to
Cherie's party tonight, which is no big
loss. But today at lunch she looked like
missing this bash would be the worst
thing that ever happened to her. (All
right, so yeah, I'm going to be there—
maybe she's just sad that she doesn't
get to hang with me all night :-))

So that's the news round here. I
don't know what's going to happen with
any of it, but I'll give you my pre-
diction: Situation #3 is going to blow
up. Big time.

Later. Don't study too hard.
                          —Andy

CHAPTER 8

Warped Version of the Truth

Ken watched Maria as she took her last bites of shrimp ravioli. She looked incredibly beautiful tonight, her ice blue top complementing her dark complexion and the low neckline showing off the rather smooth-looking expanse of skin right around her collarbone.

She glanced up at Ken at that moment, then her eyes quickly darted back down to her pasta. She began to wrap a curl of hair around her finger with one hand as she pushed her remaining food around on the plate with her other.

Unfortunately, she also looked uncomfortable. She'd been so quiet ever since they'd arrived. Usually he couldn't get Maria to shut up if he wanted to.

But as he took a sip of his Coke, the answer suddenly came to him in a rush. Maybe, just like him, she was wondering when they were going to kiss already. Maybe it was all she could think about and that's why she was acting weird. Ken smiled. He knew what that felt like.

Just talk to her about it, Ken told himself.

"Maria?" he said.

"Yes?" she asked. Her brown eyes opened wide, glittering as they always did.

His stomach fell. "Uh, do you want to try some of my pasta?" he asked. *Wuss.*

"Um, sure." Maria unwrapped her finger from her hair. "I'm always up for tasting."

"All right." He dug into his pasta, careful to twirl a good amount of linguine as well as some sausage onto his fork. And then he had an inspired idea. Just as he'd seen the lead actors do in all of those sappy romantic comedies that his mom loved to watch, Ken reached over the table with his fork, aiming right for Maria's mouth.

It turned out not to be such an easy target. Maria quickly retracted, pulling away and staring back at Ken as if he'd just grown another nose.

"What?" Ken asked. "What's wrong?"

Maria's mouth dropped open. Then she closed it. She crossed her arms over her chest, and her normally large, round eyes narrowed into impossibly slitted ovals.

"Maria?" Ken prompted, completely confused.

"Do you think we're on a date or something?" she suddenly blurted out.

Ken blinked. Did he *think?* "Yeah . . . of course I do," he said.

Maria's eyes lit up with a spark of . . . *anger?* "Just great." She threw her hands up in the air. "You could've told me," she argued. "I mean, I'd like to know when I'm going on a first date!"

"A *first* date?" Ken was shocked. Stunned. He was beyond stunned; he was . . . something he couldn't find a word to describe. He felt himself begin to sweat. Big time. "Maria, what do you think we've been doing all week?" he managed to ask at last.

Maria looked back at him for a long, silent moment, her eyes gradually opening back to their normal size. "I thought we were just spending time together, Ken. As friends. Hanging out. You know, like I do with Liz."

Like *Liz?* It felt like every ounce of blood in Ken's body rushed to his cheeks. Sweat dripped out of every possible pore. Ken looked down at his plate, shifting in his seat. Oh, man, this was such a total disaster. Ken felt like a complete fool. He wished with all his might that he could just crawl under the table and disappear through a magic door in the floor. He clenched his hands into tight, clammy fists. God, he should have known better than to think he had what it took to pull off a date with Maria.

"Ken?" she asked, her voice a little softer now.

Ken glanced up at her, his mouth completely dry. "Yeah?" he choked out.

"Do you *want* to date me?"

Did he want to date her? Of course he wanted to date her! That's what this beyond-embarrassing experience was all about, wasn't it? Well, he wasn't about to humiliate himself any more than he already had. He focused on his glass of water. "Do *you* want to?" he mumbled.

He heard Maria let out a little sigh. "I don't know," she said after a moment.

Right. Just the enthusiastic response I was hoping for. "Yeah," he muttered, fidgeting with his fork. "Me either."

A tense, heavy silence fell over them for what felt like an hour.

"Are you two done?" the waiter asked, suddenly appearing by Ken's side.

"Uh, yes," Ken told him, more than relieved for the distraction.

"Can I interest you in any of our award-winning desserts?"

"No," Ken responded quickly, without consulting Maria. "We'll just take the check."

"Very well." The waiter began to clear their plates, and Ken looked at his watch, avoiding eye contact with Maria at all costs.

They were definitely going to be early to Cherie's. But he didn't care. It would be better than sitting here for a second longer, feeling like an idiot, with his cheeks burning—award-winning desserts or not.

Conner burst into his mother's room, slamming the door open wide. As far as he was concerned, Gary didn't deserve a knock. The guy barely deserved to be alive.

Gary sat up in bed, his tiny specks of eyes filled with anger and alarm. He set the hardcover book he'd been reading aside. "Conner? What are you doing here?"

No. What the hell are you *doing here?* Conner felt sick as he stared back at Gary's sweaty face. His normally pale, pudgy cheeks were now inflamed with a slight pinkish color. The guy looked like a pig. Well, at least his looks matched his personality. Conner walked over and shoved Megan's note in his ex-stepfather's face. "Here. You happy now? She could be on her way to Mexico, for all we know."

Gary nodded in his annoyingly calm way as he read the note. As if the letter had simply said, *Went to get milk—be back soon.* Conner stormed away from him and dropped into his mother's desk chair, his leg bouncing out of control. He couldn't sit here and watch Gary act like this was no big deal. Was the jerk ever going to get a clue?

"All right, all right, don't get all worked up," Gary said, placing the piece of paper down next to him on the bed. "I'm sure she's fine. She probably just went to one of her normal hangouts."

Negative. Gary was bound to be a clueless idiot for the rest of his miserable life. Conner could have strangled him. In fact, he would have, if he wasn't so concerned with finding Megan first.

"You don't get it." Conner stomped over and snatched the note off the bed. "She's upset. She's not thinking. She could do something stupid."

Gary stood up, letting out a condescending sigh and practically rolling his eyes. "Now, listen, I know about these things from experience. In these cases—"

"She's not a case!" Conner shouted. It took every ounce of restraint that he had not to punch Gary out. "She's your daughter!"

"Arguing is not going to solve this, Conner," Gary said slowly. "Don't you think it was our arguing that made Megan so upset in the first place?"

Conner had never felt so full of frustration and rage in his life. The guy constantly spouted out his own warped version of the truth. There was no point.

Conner stalked over to his mother's desk and picked up a pad, then grabbed her silver pen. As quickly as he could, he scribbled down a list of Megan's friends. Then he ripped off the piece of paper and practically threw it at his ex-stepfather.

"Here," he said. "Call them and ask if they've seen her."

Gary glanced down at the piece of paper as it fluttered to the floor.

"That's if you care," Conner added, before bolting out of the room.

He wasn't about to wait for an answer.

Please be here, Sandy. Please be here, Conner chanted to himself forty minutes later as he drove over to Sweet Valley High's soccer field. He was running out of places to look. He'd already checked the old playground where Megan sometimes hung out with her friends, he'd run through the mall like a lunatic, and he'd stopped by Shira and Wendy's houses. No Megan anywhere.

If she wasn't here, Conner would be at a total loss. He was really starting to get scared.

He pulled his Mustang into the field's parking lot and jumped out with the car still running, rushing outside to look for her. But the dark field was empty and desolate. Not a person in sight.

Conner's shoulders collapsed. He glanced up at the star-filled night sky. "Come on," he said aloud, feeling desperate. "Where is she?" Then, feeling stupid, he quickly turned around and ran back to the car.

He slid inside and took off, his tires screeching as he slammed on the gas. But Conner had no clue where he was going. He was out of ideas.

Tia! he thought suddenly, making a quick right turn to head toward her house. She lived just a couple of blocks from him. Maybe there was a shot that she or her brothers had seen Megan.

Conner kept his eyes peeled on the sidewalk as he drove. Before he knew it, he was in front of the Ramirezes' house. He ran out of his car and up the pathway and almost smacked right into Tia, who was on her way out.

"God, Conner, what's wrong?" she asked immediately, stepping back.

"Have you seen Megan?" he said, catching his breath.

"No. Why?" Tia's eyes searched his face. "What is it? You're scaring me."

"She got into a fight with Gary and took off. I have no idea where she is."

"Is that all?" Tia grinned, slinging her mesh bag over her shoulder. "She probably just needs some time to herself. You, of all people, should understand that."

"No, Tee, this is serious," Conner snapped. "She was *really* upset. I've looked everywhere. She could've done something stupid."

"*Megan?*" Tia asked. "Megan hasn't done a stupid thing in her life."

Conner let out a short, frustrated breath. "Yeah, well, there's a first time for everything. You didn't see how she was acting tonight." His body stiffened as he wondered if Gary had bothered to pick up the phone yet. "Tee, if I don't find her soon, I'll . . . I'll—"

"Okay, okay, calm down. Let's think, then," Tia interrupted softly, grabbing both of his arms and looking up at him with concerned eyes.

"I just told you I've looked everywhere," Conner spat out. Why did everyone keep telling him to calm down? There was nothing to be calm about.

"*Oo-kay.*" Tia let go of his arms. She chewed on

the inside of her lip. "So you've gone over to Liz's?"

Conner froze. *Liz!* How could he not have thought of that? He shoved his hands in his front pockets. "No."

"Mmmm," Tia murmured. She pulled her long hair up into a bun, her dark eyes twinkling. "I guess you have a different definition of 'everywhere.'"

Conner rolled his eyes. "Come on. Not now, Tee," he muttered. Then he glanced over at his car, and his legs suddenly felt like lead. He knew what he had to do now. Drive over to Elizabeth's. There was more than a good shot that Megan was there. And an extremely good shot that Elizabeth was there. Which was exactly why Conner now felt glued to the pavement.

Tia had already turned and begun to walk over to Conner's Mustang. She glanced at Conner over her shoulder. "Well?"

Conner sighed. Finding Megan was all that mattered. The Elizabeth factor shouldn't affect anything.

Conner walked over and roughly pulled open the driver's-side door.

He could pretend all he wanted to. But he knew the Elizabeth factor always affected everything.

Jessica Wakefield

Why is it that ever since the school year started, Liz and I can't be happy at the same time? It's like some evil twin hex was put on us. I mean, here I am, sitting in my room, all giddy over Will, but it doesn't feel as special when I can't share it with my sister. And as much as I want to, I can't really lose myself in thoughts about him right now because I'm too busy thinking about the fact that Megan is in Liz's room at this very moment and how my parents will flip if they find out.

I'm really worried about Liz. I just want her to be happy.

But it would be nice if I didn't have to fall into a pit of misery in order for that to happen.

CHAPTER
Irrational Alien Beings

9

"Thanks for listening, Liz," Megan said, sitting cross-legged on Elizabeth's bed and throwing her fifth wadded-up tissue into the wicker wastepaper basket. Elizabeth handed her a clean tissue, but Megan shook her head. "I think I'm all right."

"Good," Elizabeth said, relieved that Megan had finally calmed down. "But please don't thank me." She dropped down next to her. "I'm your friend. I'll always be here to talk."

"Thanks," Megan said, then bit her lip, smiling. "I mean—"

"I know what you mean." Elizabeth laughed. "But you know what? Instead of thanking me, you could do me a favor."

"Sure," Megan said, perking up. "Anything."

Elizabeth picked the cordless phone up off the floor and placed it in Megan's lap. "Call him." When Megan gave her an annoyed look, Elizabeth quickly added, "Just so he won't worry."

Megan sighed. "Okay. But if my dad answers, I'm hanging up," she muttered, picking up the phone.

"You know, Conner thought I was in my room with the door closed when I left anyway. He might not have even noticed that I'm gone."

I hope so, Elizabeth thought as she watched Megan take a deep breath and dial. Megan had had enough grief for one night. The last thing she needed was for a worried Conner to lose it on her.

"It's busy," Megan said, clicking the phone off and tossing it onto the bed. "I keep telling Conner we need call waiting."

"Guys never understand things like that." Elizabeth glanced at her watch. It was getting late. Too late for Megan to ride her bike back home by herself—it was a long distance from Elizabeth's house to the Sandborns'. "Well, I would drive you home, except for the tiny problem that my parents would skin me alive."

"That's right! I feel so bad," Megan said, moving to the edge of the bed. "Thanks so much for letting me in when you're grounded and everything."

Elizabeth stood up, tossing her stuffed monkey at Megan's head. "What did I just say about thanking me?"

Megan ducked, and the stuffed animal hit the wall behind her. "I'm sorry! I can't help it."

"Just don't let it happen again," Elizabeth joked. She picked up the phone again, fiddling with its antenna. "Should we just hang out and try calling again in a few minutes?"

Megan shrugged. "Sounds like a plan."

"Okay." Elizabeth reached for her remote control. "You feel like watching TV?" she asked. "I don't know if there's anything good on, but—"

The doorbell rang.

Elizabeth froze midsentence. She looked at Megan, whose eyes were popped wide open, her face pale. "You don't think that's . . ." But Elizabeth didn't need to finish her sentence. Megan's freaked-out facial expression said it all.

In a flash both girls flew to the window and looked down at the Wakefields' driveway. Elizabeth felt dizzy. There it was.

Conner's Mustang.

"Oh, God," Megan said, clasping the window cushion. "He's gonna kill me."

Elizabeth swallowed. *When Mom and Dad see Conner on our doorstep,* she thought, her knees feeling weak and her belly light, I'm *the one who's dead.*

Conner wiped his sweaty palms against his jeans as he and Tia stood in front of the Wakefields' front door.

She had to be here—she just had to be. And if she wasn't, well, Elizabeth could have some ideas. She knew Megan pretty well. Then again, that would require asking Ms. Do-gooder for her help once again and—

Conner forced the thought out of his brain.

"You think I should press it again?" Tia asked.

It *did* seem like they'd been standing there for ten years. Conner was about to open his mouth to say yes when the front door swung open.

Elizabeth's mother, wearing dark, stiff-looking jeans and a crisp white blouse, stood before them. She smiled tentatively at both Tia and Conner, and her seemingly wrinkle-free forehead creased into several lines.

"Hi, Tia, Conner," she greeted them, looking from one to the other, confusion evident in her blue-green eyes. "Are you here to see Jessica? She didn't mention you were coming over."

"Actually, Mrs. Wakefield," Tia responded, "we're here to see Liz." She clutched Conner's arm. "He needs to talk to her."

Conner glanced past Mrs. Wakefield into the house, as if he was going to find Megan hiding behind Elizabeth's mother.

"Well, I'm sorry, guys," Mrs. Wakefield said. "But Liz is grounded. She's not allowed to have any guests."

Liz? Grounded? Conner's brain clouded. That made no sense whatsoever. "Uh, Mrs. Wakefield," he began awkwardly. He was never one to do well around parents. "This is kind of an emergency. I just need to talk to her for a second."

"Sorry. You'll have to wait until tomorrow," Mrs. Wakefield responded.

She had to be kidding. Conner was just about to

push the woman out of his way and go find his sister himself when he spotted Elizabeth and Megan running down the beige-carpeted stairs behind her.

Thank God! Relief washed over him. Megan was here! She was safe!

He was going to kill her.

"Megan!" he exclaimed.

Mrs. Wakefield swiveled around, her chin-length hair swinging as she did. "Liz!" she snapped. "What's going on?"

Elizabeth winced as she approached. "I'm sorry, Mom. I can explain."

Mrs. Wakefield shook her head at her daughter. "Just wrap it up," she said tersely. "Then come see me in the kitchen."

As Mrs. Wakefield stalked off, Megan gave Conner an apologetic look. "I'm really sorry, Conner," she said.

Conner reached out and pulled her into a hug. "God, Sandy. You scared me half to death. What the hell were you thinking?"

"I'm sorry," Megan repeated, pulling away. "I just had to get away from that house. I had to get away from all that fighting . . . and from Dad."

Conner's heart constricted as he took in his sister's defeated expression. She was miserable, and it was his fault. He had let her down. Well, it wasn't going to happen again. "Everything's going to be all right," he promised, clasping both of her skinny arms. "You have to trust me on that. Okay?"

Megan's eyes darted to the ground. "Okay."

"No, I'm serious," Conner said, lifting her chin with his finger so that she was forced to look at him. "You've always trusted me in the past, and you have to trust me now. I'm going to figure things out. I promise. All right?"

Megan nodded but still looked somber. "All right."

"Good." Sighing with exhaustion, Conner glanced over at Elizabeth. Her hands were by her sides, and she was watching him. He stared at her for a moment. The fact that she looked so beautiful in just a man's white V-necked T-shirt and worn gray sweatpants, her hair messily thrown up into a ponytail, suddenly really irked him. Especially considering that she was the last thing he should be thinking about at a moment like this. And was that *sympathy* in her eyes? He felt a burst of anger rise up in him out of nowhere. "I can't believe you didn't call me and let me know she was here," he said, glaring at her.

Elizabeth's mouth fell open. Her face turned pale. "I tried to, Conner, but I—"

"But you didn't?" Conner snapped.

"Don't, Conner," Megan begged, pulling on his arm. "Don't get mad at Liz! She asked me to call you, but I didn't want to. And then she finally convinced me, but the line was busy!"

"For three hours?" Conner exclaimed.

Elizabeth opened her mouth to speak, but no

words came out. Her aqua eyes clouded over. She looked like she might crumble.

For some reason, that's exactly what Conner wanted.

But then she seemed to harden. "No, Conner," Elizabeth argued back, taking a step forward and tightening the green elastic around her ponytail. "That's not what happened at all."

"Please, Liz. Spare me your lame explanations."

"Okay, you know what? I think everyone needs to calm down just a little bit," Tia announced suddenly, stepping in between Conner and Elizabeth. "All that matters is that Megan's fine. No need to go Springer on each other."

"Whatever," Conner said. "Let's just go home."

Megan sighed. "But Conner, Liz was only trying to help."

"Yeah," he muttered. He leveled Elizabeth with a glare. "And she did a great job."

Elizabeth's eyes blurred with tears as she watched Conner's Mustang peel off down the road. She let out a shaky sigh. That was it. It was over. Conner was still angry with her, and there was nothing she could do about it . . . except hope that he and Megan would be okay.

The worst part of it all was that he was right. Elizabeth *could have* snuck away from Megan at any moment and called Conner herself. Then he wouldn't have had to worry, to chase around searching for her. *How could I be so stupid?* she wondered, closing the front door.

Then again, she had only been looking out for Megan. An angry, indignant flush crept over Elizabeth's face. Conner didn't have to be so hard on her. If he'd only given her a chance to explain . . . Why did she always let him get to her, even when he was clearly being unreasonable? Here she had gone to the lengths of sneaking Megan into her house and—

Elizabeth's stomach fell. She looked at the kitchen, and her knees felt like they might give out. *Mom,* she remembered.

Elizabeth took a deep breath and headed for the kitchen. *Mom'll understand,* she comforted herself as she walked. *I couldn't have turned Megan away when she was so worked up. Mom will realize that.*

But as soon as Elizabeth took one step onto the cold, terra-cotta kitchen floor, she knew she was in for it. Her mom was straightening up their impeccably clean kitchen, scrubbing the spotless countertop with a blue-and-white-checked dish towel. She didn't look at Elizabeth.

"I can't believe you smuggled a guest into this house," she said flatly.

"Mom, I'm sorry," Elizabeth said, taking a few tiny, tentative steps forward. "Megan was really upset. She had nowhere else to go."

Mrs. Wakefield continued to wipe the counter. "Then why didn't you just come ask me if it was all right for her to come in?"

Maybe because I was afraid of how you'd react, Elizabeth thought, fidgeting with the hem of her T-shirt. "Because I didn't want to bother you and Dad," she explained. "Megan was hysterical. I just wanted to calm her down."

"Elizabeth, please!" Mrs. Wakefield threw her hands up in the air, her voice raising several notches. "We specifically told you that you weren't allowed to have any friends over, and you disobeyed us! Don't try to give me some explanation!"

Elizabeth blinked. *Some* explanation? "But Mom," she protested, walking up behind her. "This is what really happened. I—"

"I never thought that we'd have to deal with this sort of behavior from you," her mom interrupted. "I don't know why you're suddenly doing this, but we're not going to allow it. Do you hear me?"

Do you *hear* me *is a better question,* Elizabeth thought as she stared at her mother's slim back. It was as if her mother's body had been taken over by some alien being. Some completely *irrational* alien being. At a complete loss, Elizabeth glanced around the room and saw that her sister stood in the doorway, watching them. She was hugging herself, her eyebrows knit together in concern.

"Don't worry," Elizabeth mouthed to Jessica. She

felt a little stronger now that she knew her sister was there to support her.

"Mom," she said, "it didn't happen the way you—"

"I don't want to hear anything more from you tonight!" Mrs. Wakefield cut her off.

"Mom! Stop yelling," Jessica called out. "Liz didn't do anything wrong. Megan came to her for help."

Elizabeth gave her sister a small smile. It was odd having Jessica defend her instead of the reverse. But now her mother had to believe her. She had to understand.

Mrs. Wakefield turned to Jessica. "You *knew* that Megan was over even though Liz was grounded?"

Or not, Elizabeth thought, her heart sinking.

"Well, yeah, I mean, I . . . yeah," Jessica began, completely flustered. "But you have to understand. Megan was really upset and—"

"That's it!" Mrs. Wakefield sliced her hand through the air. Elizabeth took a step back. She had never seen her mother act like this in her entire life. "Both of you, go up to your rooms."

Jessica's mouth fell open. "But Mom, I—"

"Now," Mrs. Wakefield ordered. "And Elizabeth, you're grounded for one more week."

Elizabeth saw Jessica jump at her mother's tone. She took a few steps out of the room and waited for Elizabeth just outside the door. But Elizabeth couldn't have moved if she wanted to.

"Let's go, Elizabeth—I don't want to have to tell you again," Mrs. Wakefield said. She let out a heavy sigh. "I'm very disappointed in you."

Elizabeth slowly turned around. What more could she say? As she trudged out of the room and up the stairs, Jessica in tow, she felt dizzy and light-headed.

Talk about being disappointed, she thought, her hand tracing the carved wooden banister. *I never thought I wouldn't be able to talk to my mother.*

"Hey, Conner, wanna hang out for a sec?" Tia asked as she climbed out of the Mustang.

Conner sighed. *Here it comes,* he thought, slamming the car door. But he knew he had no choice. Tia would never leave him alone before she said what she wanted to say. "Go on inside," he told Megan. "I'll be there in a minute."

Megan nodded. "All right." She gave Conner a quick hug. "And I'm sorry . . . again." She jogged off toward the front door.

"So." Tia linked her arm around Conner's, leading him toward the sidewalk. "Don't you think you better go and apologize to Liz?"

"Funny." Conner broke away from her. "Just what I thought you'd say."

"Oh, yeah?" Tia dropped down onto the curb. She raised one eyebrow as she looked up at him. "Maybe that's because you know I'm right. Your conscience—that is, if you have one—is telling you the same thing."

"Or maybe it's because you're very predictable," Conner argued, smirking.

Tia rolled her eyes. She rifled through her bag, searching until she pulled out her keys. "Conner, I'm serious. You owe Liz a major apology."

"Why?" Conner squinted out into the distance, focusing on nothing in particular. *Just get through this with Tia, and then you won't have to think about Liz again tonight—or ever.* "Because I was driving around like a maniac looking for my sister when all Liz had to do was call?"

"God, Conner!" Tia stood back up, pointing at him with her keys. "All Liz has ever done is be there for you, and all you ever do is treat her like crap. Don't you see that? She took care of Megan tonight." She bent down and picked her bag up off the curb. "You're lucky to have Liz around. And I don't know if there's anything even *left* to salvage, but if you know what's good for you, you better try."

Conner was silent. He kicked at the ground. "You know what I think, Tee?" he said finally.

She adjusted her bag on her shoulder. "What?"

"I think you should mind your own business."

"Ugh!" Tia threw her hands up in the air. "You are so annoying sometimes! Conner, you know you're wrong. Deal with it." She turned and headed for the rear of his house and the shortcut that led to her own.

Conner just turned his back on her and stood there for a moment, staring at the quiet, empty street. She was such a drama queen sometimes. But then something made him glance over his shoulder. He watched Tia's tiny frame disappear behind the bushes, her long ponytail swinging behind her. From this distance she didn't look much different from how she had looked when she was ten. He started to think about how long he and Tia had been friends, how many times she had freaked out on him in the past.

He closed his eyes. And remembered how many times she'd been right.

Maria Slater

<u>Reasons for and Against Going Out with Ken</u>
<u>For</u>

He makes me feel important.

He's cute—make that adorable.

We always have fun together.

He understands me.

Okay . . . yes, I could be attracted to him. Maybe. Probably.

All right, I <u>am</u> attracted to him.

<u>Against</u>

We're friends. (Yes, I know, that can be a good basis for a relationship. But it can also screw everything up.)

He might not be over Olivia.

He . . .

I . . .

Um . . .

"Nice place," Ken mumbled as he and Maria walked from his car and up the hilly driveway to Cherie Reese's Spanish-villa-style house.

"Yeah," Maria agreed. She couldn't wait to get inside. Ever since she had confronted Ken at Enzo's, things had been beyond awkward between them. Maria could probably count the amount of words that had passed between them in the past half hour. Now all she wanted to do was get to the party, find one of her friends, and pretend this evening's events had never occurred.

Well, maybe not never, Maria amended as they neared Cherie's front door. It wasn't that she was repulsed by the idea of going out with Ken . . . not at all. In fact, she was getting more and more used to the thought of it. *Maybe.* It was just that she couldn't get over how he'd handled the whole situation. As if Maria was supposed to magically read his mind and realize that they were now dating, even though he'd never discussed the subject once! And when she'd called him on it, when she'd asked him to simply explain his emotions, he'd turned into prehistoric man, capable only of grunts and groans. How could she go out with someone like that?

Ken reached for the shiny brass knocker on the huge wooden door, and the door swung right open. Ken and Maria glanced at each other and shrugged, then they both stepped inside.

Maria gripped the handle of her woven straw bag. There was a grand total of about twenty people—none of them Maria's friends—hanging out in Cherie's high-ceilinged, airy living room ahead. She glanced at her watch. They were definitely on the early side. *And it could be a long time until Tia and Andy get here,* she realized, her stomach sinking into her flower-patterned clogs.

She glanced over at Ken, who was nervously scanning the room himself. "So," he began, lifting his eyebrows.

Maria nodded, relaxing a little. "So." Maybe Ken was going to take this opportunity to really talk to her—to try to work things through. Maybe he'd actually developed some social skills in the past couple of minutes.

"Uh . . . nice place," he said—again.

Or maybe not. Maria had to hold herself back from shaking him silly. Was this his idea of romancing a girl? It was more like a surefire way to lose a good friend.

Then she saw Ken's eyes come alive when he

spotted someone across the room. "Hey, Wilkins!" he called out, looking as excited as if Michael Jordan were suddenly before him.

Todd turned around and smiled when he saw Ken. "Hey, Matthews," he called back. "Dallas, Ken's here," he yelled over at Aaron, who was rifling through the CDs by the extremely high-tech-looking stereo unit.

Before Maria even realized it was happening, Ken made a beeline straight for his buddies, and she was standing there by herself in Cherie Reese's entryway, feeling like a total loser.

Lovely. This was what she got for trying to break out and be social for once. Maria took a step onto the enormous southwestern rug that covered most of the living-room floor, glancing around while she prayed to see a familiar face. But the only other people she knew there—aside from the football guys— were Melissa Fox, Gina Cho, and Cherie herself. At the moment the three of them were sitting on a leather beige sofa in the middle of the room, drinking out of wineglasses.

Maria sighed as she reviewed her options. (1) She could continue to stand by herself until her friends came, passing the time by counting tiles in the white-and-light-blue-tiled floor of the entryway. (2) She could go talk to Melissa, Gina, and Cherie until her friends came and ignore the fact that she thought all of them were snobby brats. Or (3), she could leave the party altogether, but since Ken had driven her, she'd have to call a cab or something.

Doesn't look like I have many viable options, Maria thought, taking a deep breath and heading over to Melissa and company.

She shook her head as she walked. *Good thing I'm an actress,* she thought. *'Cause I'm going to need my acting skills to be friendly to these girls.*

Jessica plopped down on her bed, smiling euphorically after having just gotten off the phone with Will. She'd been pretty bummed when she'd called him since she had to tell him not to come over tonight, given the wrathful mood that her mother was in. But the teasing sound of his deep voice had cheered her up instantly. Talking to Will on the phone was almost as good as hanging out with him in person. Now, if they could just figure out a way to *kiss* over the phone . . .

Jessica sat up at the sound of Elizabeth banging around in her room. It sounded like she was moving furniture or something. What could she be doing?

Jessica hopped up and headed for Elizabeth's room, hoping she could figure out a way to cheer up her sister. "Hey, Liz?" she called, knocking on her door.

"Come in," Elizabeth called back.

Jessica opened the door to see Elizabeth putting on her cranberry capri pants. Was her sister going completely nuts? "Liz? What are you doing?" Jessica whispered, quickly closing the door behind her.

"Getting dressed," Elizabeth returned as she slipped her feet into a pair of black mules.

"Right," Jessica said. "I got that. But has it slipped your mind that you're grounded . . . like, three times?"

"No." Elizabeth checked her reflection in the large, oval-shaped mirror above her dresser. She ran a brush through her hair. "But I'm going to Cherie's party anyway."

"What?" Jessica exclaimed, then put her hand over her mouth. "What?" she repeated, whispering this time. "Are you crazy? Mom and Dad'll kill you!"

"Well, you know what? Mom and Dad have totally lost it. So I don't care what they do." Elizabeth leaned in to the mirror, going to work on her makeup.

For a split second Jessica just stared at her in shock. Clearly her sister had gone insane. She quickly reached over and grabbed the mascara wand out of Elizabeth's hand.

"Liz, I completely understand why you're mad," she began. "I do. But don't go. It's not worth it. What if they find out somehow? You'll be grounded for life!"

"I don't care." Elizabeth shook her head as she grabbed her beaded purse up off her desk, throwing her worn leather wallet into it. "I mean, they've trusted me my whole life, and now it's like I'm back in diapers. It makes no sense."

"They're not making sense?" Jessica said, putting the wand back in its container. "Hello? Look at you."

Elizabeth ignored her, rushing through the room as if she was on a party-going mission—as if attending Cherie's little fete was going to make or break her. When she ran over to her night table to grab her phone, Jessica followed right behind.

"Liz, if they catch you tonight, they're just going to treat you even worse," Jessica said.

"Well, I won't let them," Elizabeth insisted, dialing the phone. "I'm almost an adult. I'm *not* moving backward."

"But Liz—"

Elizabeth held up a hand, signaling for Jessica to be quiet. Jessica shut her mouth. What else could she do? It was obvious her sister wouldn't be listening to her anytime soon.

"Hey, Andy," Elizabeth said into the phone. "It's Liz. . . . Fine. Listen, it turns out I am going to Cherie's after all. . . . Yes . . . Could you pick me up? . . . My corner? Ten minutes? Thanks. Bye."

Elizabeth hit the off button on the receiver. Jessica stared at her sister in stunned silence once again as she pulled on her little black cardigan. She had never seen Elizabeth so . . . *determined*. Not even about school. And here she was, dead set on risking life and limb to go to some lame party.

"Will you cover for me, Jess?" Elizabeth asked, walking over to the door.

Jessica blinked, experiencing a distorted sort of déjà vu. How many times had she asked the very same thing of Elizabeth? "Um, yeah, sure. Of course," Jessica told her.

Elizabeth nodded. "Thanks." She gave Jessica a quick peck on the cheek. Then she was out the door.

As Jessica wiped Elizabeth's lipstick off her cheek, she numbly glanced around and noticed something even more freaky than the scene she'd just witnessed. Various clothes lay thrown across the floor, most of the drawers in the mahogany dresser had been left open, and makeup bottles and barrettes cluttered Elizabeth's desk.

Elizabeth's room was a complete mess.

Something was *very* wrong.

Come on, Conner. Where are you? Elizabeth wondered as she stood next to Maria at Cherie's party. She scanned the entire crowded living room, keeping her eyes peeled for him and not really listening as Maria talked on and on.

Okay, so Elizabeth's sudden out-of-control urge to disobey her parents had *not* been the only thing propelling her to this party. Her intense, rather pressing desire to talk to Conner and make him understand what had happened tonight also played a part. She knew that Conner had more steam to let off, and she'd been certain that this was exactly where he would come.

Well, she'd been exactly wrong. Conner was nowhere in sight.

". . . Can you believe him? Look how he's talking to Gina! What's *that* about?" Maria was saying.

"Huh? Oh, I don't know," Elizabeth responded, fidgeting with her necklace, totally clueless as to who the "him" was that Maria was referring to.

"Me either," Maria agreed. "What does he think he's trying to prove? I mean . . ."

Elizabeth stopped processing Maria's words as she fell back into her own thoughts. *What am I doing here?* she wondered suddenly as she glanced around the party. People downed their drinks, danced like fools, and tripped all over each other. A large portion of the football team and their hangers-on were playing quarters on the coffee table. *Whoo-pee.* This was *so* boring. All she'd done since she arrived was talk to Maria. She loved Maria and everything, but she didn't need to sneak out of the house to hang out with her. She could do that any night of the week.

But now here she was, at this stupid party, watching her drunk classmates behave like idiots, putting up with horrible, extremely loud dance music and sure to face capital punishment from her parents on her return home, and for what?

"You know what? You're totally right," Maria burst out suddenly, nudging Elizabeth.

She looked at her friend. *Right?* she wondered. *About what?*

Maria pulled down on her pale blue shirt, then made an effort to adjust her hair. "He's just doing this to annoy me. Well, I'm going to show him!"

Elizabeth's mouth fell open as she watched Maria stalk off for the other end of the room, her clogs stomping over the rug. Maria was definitely worked up about something, but since Elizabeth had barely been listening to her, she didn't know what it was. She did know one thing, though. Now she wasn't only bored at this party. She was bored *and* alone.

Perfect. Elizabeth sighed. None of her other friends were here. After Andy had dropped her off, he'd driven over to pick up Tia, and the two of them still hadn't showed up yet.

I guess I could go talk to Todd, she thought, spotting him walking into the kitchen. But that idea was pretty unappealing. All of their conversations since their breakup were so fake and forced, and tonight the last thing Elizabeth felt like doing was making an effort.

"Refills, everyone! Refills!"

Elizabeth turned to see Cherie heading toward her, giggling and handing out drinks in plastic cups from a silver tray. "They're my own special concoction," she told Jon Waller, a senior, as she laughed flirtatiously. "I think you'll like it!"

Elizabeth rolled her eyes. Cherie was obviously

smashed, what with her overly giddy behavior and her disheveled appearance—her red hair was a tangled mess, and both of her black tank-top straps were falling off her shoulders, revealing her lavender bra.

"Hey, perk up, Wakefield!" Cherie was suddenly in Elizabeth's face. "It *is* a party." Cherie handed Elizabeth a drink. "We're all here to have fun, aren't we?"

Elizabeth glanced down at the purplish-colored drink as Cherie bounced off. She couldn't stand Cherie, but the girl did have a point. And Elizabeth *had* gone to the trouble of sneaking out of the house to get here.

Elizabeth shrugged. *Well . . . might as well have a good time.*

In one swift movement she downed her drink.

She crinkled up her nose at the taste, then cracked a small smile.

Let the fun begin!

". . . and out *there* is where Cherie and I used to play with our Barbie dolls," Gina went on, giggling and pointing with her long, red-painted nail at the backyard. "We really loved those dolls. Funny, right?"

"Uh, yeah. That's pretty funny," Ken responded, glancing at his watch. Man, he had been here for hours, and all he'd done so far was have pointless conversation after pointless conversation. "You know what, Gina? I gotta go to the bathroom," he said.

"Oh, sure. There's one right through the kitchen," Gina told him, flipping her dark hair over her shoulder.

"Okay, thanks." Ken nodded, turning around.

"See you later!" Gina called after him.

Ken glanced back and waved, then headed across the room toward the kitchen. He didn't actually have to go to the bathroom. He'd just needed an excuse to get away from Gina . . . and to find Maria.

All he wanted to do was talk to her. She was the only reason he was here in the first place. And at first he'd been really hurt—not to mention humiliated—by her reaction in the restaurant. But now that he'd had some time and distance to cool down and think everything over, he realized that the whole thing *was* sort of his fault. He should have asked her out on a date rather than assumed that she'd know what his intentions were. Ken shook his head. He was such a bumbling idiot. He never did anything right. And he certainly would never understand girls.

But he did know one thing: He wasn't about to lose Maria—as a friend or otherwise. She was too important to him. Too special. He smiled slightly as a trace of hope came over him. Maria hadn't said flat out that she *didn't* want to go out with him, so maybe—

Then Ken saw something that made him freeze. Maria was dancing a couple of feet away from him—with Aaron Dallas. And she was smiling at Aaron. *Flirtatiously.*

Ken's nostrils flared as he watched Maria sway her hips. What was she doing—the forbidden dance or something? And with Aaron Dallas, of all people? She was, like, five inches taller than the guy.

"Ken Matthews! You wanna dance?"

Ken glanced down to see Cherie grinning up at him, holding a drink in one hand and looking like she might tip over at any second.

Ken grabbed her drink-free arm. "Yeah," he told her tightly, glaring over at Maria and Aaron, "I would."

Lila Fowler

Why I Think Elizabeth Wakefield Is Losing It

All right, first of all I saw Liz walking out of Mr. Valasquez's office on Monday. Elizabeth Wakefield—Miss Straight-A Student, Miss Perfection Personified! Can you believe it? They only send you to Mr. V. if you have emotional problems or if you're a delinquent or something.

And lately Liz is always wearing Jessica's clothes. How do I know? Because I know Jessica's wardrobe inside and out. Trust me, Liz has been digging into her sister's closet. Don't get me wrong, she's still not dressing stylishly or anything—Jessica doesn't exactly live on the cutting edge of fashion these days. But still, she wears these sexy things that she wouldn't have been caught dead in last year.

If that's not enough to convince you, I overheard Liz telling Maria that she's <u>grounded</u>. Perfect Elizabeth Wakefield, grounded! I can't get over that. And get this: She <u>snuck</u> out of her house to come to Cherie's party!

And now, to top it all off, Liz looks like she's drunk! How am I so sure? Well, to begin with, the fact that she's dancing like an idiot right now is one clear sign.

I don't know what's going on with her, but I'll tell you one thing—if Liz Wakefield does lose it, no one will be as happy as me.

CHAPTER 11
Rebel, Rebel

For what felt like the hundredth time that night Conner raced his car up the street. So far, practically his entire evening had been spent in his Mustang.

When he finally reached Elizabeth's house, he trudged up to the front door and rang the bell, hoping she'd be the one to answer. Conner did not want to deal with her mother again.

The door opened, and an agitated-looking Mrs. Wakefield stood before him in a forest green terry-cloth bathrobe.

Of course. Just my luck.

"Conner?" she asked, pulling on the bathrobe's belt to close it more tightly around her waist. "Can I help you?"

"Um, yeah." Conner shifted his weight from one foot to the other. "I'm sorry to bother you again, Mrs. Wakefield. I know Liz is grounded and everything, but I really need to talk to her—for just a few minutes."

Mrs. Wakefield crossed her arms over her chest. "Why? Has she smuggled somebody *else* upstairs?"

Conner laughed. Mrs. Wakefield didn't. Conner cleared his throat. "Uh, no, she hasn't," he said. "I just really need to talk to her."

"Well, I'm sorry." Mrs. Wakefield shook her head. "But as I told you earlier, it'll have to wait until to-morrow."

"But if I could just—," Conner began to argue.

Mrs. Wakefield put up a hand to silence him. "I'm sorry," she said again. "I'm not going to change my mind on this. . . . Good night."

Conner let out a sigh. He took a step backward. "Yeah," he said, running a hand through his hair. "Good night."

Mrs. Wakefield closed the door, and Conner turned to head back to his car. He couldn't believe how strict Elizabeth's mom was. Especially consider-ing the fact that Elizabeth was such a goody-goody. How could her mother not trust her? *No wonder Liz wanted to live with us.*

"Conner!" a female voice hissed out.

He whipped around. Where did that come from? *Who* did that come from? Conner scanned the front yard.

"Conner! Up here!"

He glanced up and there Elizabeth was, hanging out of a second-story window. He took a step closer, getting a better look at her face as the moonlight fell across it. Conner squinted, taking in her features. On second thought . . .

"Jessica?" he called tentatively, just to make sure.

"Liz snuck out to go to that party over at Cherie Reese's," Jessica explained in a hoarse whisper.

Conner shoved his hands in his front pockets, confused. "She did?" he whispered back. Sneaking out to go to a party seemed very un-Liz-like. But then, her mom seemed like a total dictator. Maybe Elizabeth had to sneak out to have any fun.

"Yes! And she was all upset when she left. I'm really worried." Jessica stuck her head a little farther out the window. "Would you mind just going there and making sure she's okay?"

Conner looked at the grass. Apologizing to Elizabeth was one thing; chasing after her at some party was another. Then again, he realized, *he* was probably the reason that Elizabeth was so upset. *No*, Conner thought, not allowing himself to feel guilty. *It's not my fault that she's overly sensitive.* He glanced back up at Jessica. "If you're so worried, why don't *you* just go and look for her?"

"Because," she continued to whisper, sounding exasperated, "I have to stay up here and make noise so my parents don't realize she's gone. You know, cover for her."

"Oh." Conner nodded. "Right."

"Please, Conner?" Jessica begged. "My parents are going to kill her."

Conner's jaw clenched. The last thing he needed was for Elizabeth to get into trouble because she was mad at *him*. "Okay," he told Jessica, taking a step backward. "I'll go. But I'm not promising anything."

"Thank you!" Jessica said.

Conner simply turned around. As he walked back to his car, he shook his head, kicking at the loose gravel in the driveway.

Apparently his night of hunting down distressed females wasn't quite over.

"Tequila!" Elizabeth called out, singing along with the rest of the people dancing around her.

She laughed, turning to whoever she was dancing with—she couldn't quite remember who that was—and found that she wasn't really dancing with anyone in particular.

Oh, well! Elizabeth thought, swiveling back around and moving her body with the beat of the music. She threw her hands up in the air, twirling. This was so much fun! She felt so . . . free!

"Tequila!" she shouted out again, then covered her mouth with her hand, giggling. *Oops!* It wasn't quite time to yell that out yet. . . .

"Liz!"

Elizabeth jumped as she felt two hands on her shoulders. Then she saw that those hands were connected to Andy. And Andy was standing right next to Tia.

Hey, she thought, scrunching her eyebrows together and seeing her friends' faces in a whole new, alcohol-induced light, *Andy's kinda cute. And he and Tia would make a good couple.*

"Liz?" Tia asked, stepping closer to her. "Are you in there?"

"Of course I'm with you!" she exclaimed, hugging both of them. "I'm always with you! When did you get here?"

Tia pulled away from Elizabeth. She placed one hand on her miniskirt-clad hip. "Just in time to take *you* home."

Take me home? That was insane! It wasn't even close to going-home time. Elizabeth shook her head, continuing to dance. "What do you mean? I'm not going anywhere. I'm dancing!"

"Uh, yeah, Liz, we can see that," Tia said, clearing her throat. "And we can also see that you've tried some of Cherie's special recipes."

"What?" Elizabeth gasped—perhaps a bit too dramatically. She stopped dancing abruptly . . . and the room kept spinning. And spinning. "I have not!" she protested. Andy and Tia's faces blurred before her. Was the room ever going to stay still? "Okay, maybe I have. But who cares? I'm just having fun!"

"And tomorrow you'll be having a hangover," Andy chimed in, his face suddenly coming sharply into focus. Elizabeth stared into his amused blue eyes. Wow. He really was handsome. *If Tia doesn't take him, I will,* she thought, biting her lip.

161

Elizabeth tugged on his arm. "Come on, Andy, dance with me!"

"Hold up, Britney Spears." Andy didn't budge an inch. "Cheesy party songs are not my thing."

"Party pooper!" she exclaimed. Her eyes settled on a hot El Carro guy who was getting down in the center of the room. Now, *he* could dance. Elizabeth started to boogie toward him.

She tried to, at least. But her body met with great resistance. *Does drinking make you feel sluggish?* Elizabeth wondered. Then she realized that both Andy and Tia were actually holding her back, each of them pulling on one of her arms. She looked back and forth at them in confusion. Why didn't they want her to dance? They never cared when she danced before.

"Come on, Liz. We're not kidding," Tia said, getting right in her face. "It's time for you to go home."

Elizabeth couldn't believe her ears. Since when were these two the fun patrol? They were usually the ones *instigating* the fun. "You guys, chill out," she said. "It's a party!"

Elizabeth saw Andy and Tia share a look of exasperation. Man, what was their problem tonight? They were being so lame.

"Liz, you *need* to go home. You'll regret this tomorrow." Tia stared into Elizabeth's eyes. "Trust me. I've been there."

Andy let go of her arm and stood next to Tia.

"She has. Trust *me*." Tia elbowed him in the ribs. "Ow!" he exclaimed.

Yup, she thought, shaking her head. *They really would make a perfect couple.* She giggled. "I appreciate you guys looking out for me. I really, really do. But I'm fine. Okay?" She pulled herself out of Tia's grasp and stepped backward. Her foot slipped out of her mule as she did so, causing her to stumble—and to nearly fall flat on her butt. "Really," she added, trying to regain her balance.

"Right," Tia said sarcastically. "Uh-huh. Come on, Liz, there's no use in arguing. We're taking you home, and that's final."

"We're not going to leave your side until you agree," Andy put in.

Elizabeth's eyes bulged. She looked from Tia to Andy and back again. And again. Then she began to feel dizzy, so she stopped.

She looked ahead at the blur of dancing people. They were all having so much fun. This was just wrong! Her one night of freedom and her *friends* of all people were stopping her from enjoying it? She wanted to protest some more, but when she looked back at Tia and Andy, neither of them looked like they were going to budge. "Fine," she told them finally, sighing.

"Cool." Tia hugged her. "You'll thank us in the morning, I promise."

Whatever, Elizabeth thought. But as she hugged

163

Tia, she caught a glimpse of the glass door that led outside. She smiled as she watched people head out into the backyard. Suddenly she had a brilliant idea.

She pulled away from her friend. "Tee?" she said. "Is it okay if I go to the bathroom before we leave?"

Tia laughed. "I think we can allow that."

Elizabeth grinned again. There was no way she was leaving this party.

"I'm going to grab another drink. Want one?" Aaron asked Maria as the lame song they'd been dancing to came to an end.

"No, thanks," Maria told him, trying very hard *not* to roll her eyes.

Aaron flashed her a toothy smile. "All right. But when I come back, it's salsa time." He turned and trotted off.

Salsa? Oh God, please. Maria held a hand up to her throbbing head. She was more than relieved to be rid of Aaron, but with him gone, she was now left to just glance around the party by herself . . . and look for Ken.

To say she'd been bored when she was dancing with Aaron would have been a huge understatement, not to mention that she was sick of the way she and Ken were avoiding each other. The truth was, *he* was the person who she wanted to hang out with at this party, and no one else.

Why couldn't Ken be just a little more normal?

Maria wondered, her eyes searching the packed room. *Why couldn't he have actually asked me out on a date . . . or at least not gotten all weird when I asked him how he felt about me?* She shook her head. *Why couldn't he—*

Dance with Cherie Reese? Maria almost lost it right then and there, smack in the middle of the party. Ken was *dancing!* With Cherie Reese!

Maria had several problems with this. First of all, Ken did not dance. *Ever.* And second, Cherie was all over him, rubbing her obnoxious little body all over his. Not only was that gross; it was, well—Maria did *not* enjoy watching Ken dance with another girl.

Maria put her hands on her hips, fuming. *Just what does he think he's doing?* she thought. *If he's doing this to piss me off, well . . . well . . . it's working!* As Cherie reached up and encircled her pale arms around Ken's neck, Maria felt like she was going to be sick.

Without so much as a second thought, Maria stomped over to Ken and Cherie. She tapped Ken's arm.

He turned around, his blue eyes opening wide when he saw her. "Maria."

"Hi, Maria." Cherie giggled. "Having fun?"

"Great time," Maria snapped at her. She looked at Ken. "We need to talk," she told him tightly, just as the song came to an abrupt end.

A half smile crossed Ken's lips. Maria blinked.

What was *that* for? "Excuse me," he said to Cherie as a slow song started up. "Maria and I need to . . . dance."

Maria's mouth dropped open. *Dance?* What was he talking about? And why was he looking at her so strangely?

"Sure," Cherie chirped. "See you guys later!" She bounced off into the throng of dancing people.

Maria's mouth continued to hang open as Ken took her hand and pulled her into his arms. "But Ken," she began. "We need to—"

"Dance," he interrupted, wrapping his arms around her waist and sending an unexpected wave of goose bumps over her entire body. "I know."

"Ken, I . . ." Maria's voice trailed off. Suddenly she didn't know what to say. She wasn't even sure that she was capable of speaking if she wanted to. And after just a second of dancing with Ken, she didn't *want* to say anything. She was too caught up in the moment. Too choked up from the enormous wave of emotion that had overcome her out of nowhere.

Her heart beat erratically as Ken hugged her tight, their bodies swaying together. He brought his hands up to her shoulders, softly running his fingers down her bare arms. She shivered.

And then, without thinking, she rested her cheek on his firm shoulder. . . . It just felt so natural. She let out a shaky breath, comforted by his scent of detergent mingled with a hint of cologne and soothed by the feel of his soft cotton sweater against her face.

All of Maria's senses felt magnified, intensified . . . as if she'd never felt anything so deeply before.

And then she closed her eyes.

Who knew that dancing with Ken could feel so wonderful, so secure . . . so perfect? She never wanted this song to end.

But of course, it did.

Maria opened her eyes as Ken pulled away slightly.

"Maria?" he said, staring down at her.

"Yes?" she croaked, her voice shaky—her *whole body* shaky.

"I'm going to kiss you now," he told her, pushing a curl of her hair away from her face. He broke into a smile. "I wanted to tell you first—to make sure we're clear on the subject."

Maria smiled as her heart slammed against her rib cage. "Yes," she whispered. "We're clear."

Every cell in Maria's body tingled as their lips intertwined. The kiss was soft, and gentle, and exhilarating.

In a word—magic.

"Come on, Liz, jump in!"

"But I don't have a bathing suit!" Elizabeth laughed, trying very hard to keep her balance. Standing in place was getting harder and harder to do.

She was a couple of feet from Cherie's kidney-shaped pool, where Conner's friend Evan—as well as a bunch of other people from school—were swimming. But since it was so dark and since she was still feeling kind of dizzy, Elizabeth could only concentrate on Evan's face at the moment.

"Who cares?" a girl called out. "Swim in your underwear! I am!"

"My underwear?" Elizabeth laughed again, her foot slipping out of her shoe for the hundredth time that night. "No way!"

"Don't worry, it's dark out here," Evan told her. "No one can see a thing once you're in the water."

"It's warm . . . ," another guy taunted.

"Really?" Elizabeth gave up on standing altogether and dropped down into the cool grass. She stared at the pool. The water was shimmering in the moonlight. It *did* look inviting. . . .

"It feels great, Liz, really," Evan promised.

Which underwear did I put on tonight anyway? Elizabeth wondered. *That new silky pair? Or the old pink ones—with the hole in them?*

"Come on, Liz, live a little!" somebody shouted out.

Elizabeth sat up straight. That was all the encouragement she needed. "All right, I'm coming!" she exclaimed, slipping out of her shoes.

She was just standing up, about to take off her pants, when a bunch of people jumped out of the pool, running crazily in all directions. "Hey. Where's everyone going?" she yelled.

Then she heard them. Police sirens.

And they were getting louder. And louder.

The police! Elizabeth froze, her heart pounding out of control. Panicking, she looked around the dark backyard, hoping to see one of her friends.

"Evan?" she called out.

No response. And none of the dark shadows dashing away looked like anyone she knew. *I have to get out of here,* Elizabeth realized, the sirens now sounding like they were only yards away.

Now.

Will Simmons

Jessica:
- Is gorgeous.
- She's funny.
- She's carefree.
- We get along really well.
- I think she likes me a lot.
- I really like her. Think I could love her.

Melissa:
- Known her so long that I can't objectively say what she looks like. But yeah, she's very pretty.
- Has a . . . different sense of humor.
- Not carefree. Definitely not.
- Melissa understands me better than anyone else.
- No one will ever love me as much as Melissa does.
- I love her. No, I'm not in love with her. But still, I'll always love her.

CHAPTER

12

The Scene of the Crime

What the hell am I doing? Conner wondered as he hit the brakes, coming to a stop sign. Elizabeth could take care of herself. It wasn't his fault that she went all rebel and snuck out of her house. He almost wanted to turn around and just drive home.

But something—whether it was Tia's nagging voice playing inside his head, the memory of the pained look that he'd seen in Elizabeth's blue-green eyes earlier that night, or even his *own* nagging little voice—*something* caused him to keep going and turn down Cherie's road.

And into complete chaos.

Conner slowly drove over to Cherie's house. From the bottom of her uphill driveway he could see police cars parking at the top. Tons of kids were running for their cars as the cops jumped out of theirs, shining their huge flashlights everywhere.

Ducking his head, Conner tried to make out the identity of the running bodies from his car window. A number of the kids were on their way down the front yard, almost home free to the bottom of the driveway. There was no way Elizabeth was still here. She would have run at the first sound of a siren. Besides, she wasn't his responsibility.

Conner was about to pull away, wanting to get away from the cops as soon as possible, when a flashlight momentarily illuminated a familiar glint of shiny blond hair.

No, it couldn't be. But it was. That blond hair was attached to a *very* familiar-looking body. A body that was now *stumbling* down the driveway.

Conner's stomach turned over. She was drunk—or at least buzzed and scared. If the cops snagged her, she'd be toast.

Conner slammed on the gas, whipping his car around the corner and parking it behind a hedge where the police couldn't see. Then he jumped out and headed for the bushes lining Cherie's house, cursing the whole way.

Man, he thought, rushing to get to Elizabeth before the cops did. *How stupid is she?*

Oh God, oh God, oh God, Elizabeth chanted silently as she ran down the sloping front yard, panting, her shoes in her hands. *Please don't let them catch me. I swear I'll never sneak out again.*

"Stop!" an angry-sounding, deep voice called out.

Oh God, Elizabeth repeated, shaking. *Was that for me?*

Suddenly she was blinded by a bright beam of light, and she froze. Fear overtook Elizabeth, sapping

172

her body of any strength and sobering her up in an instant. She was just about to drop to her knees and surrender when someone grabbed her by the arm, pulling her through an opening in the bushes before she even had time to process what was happening.

Then all of a sudden she was standing on the side of the road, being led to . . . an old Mustang.

Elizabeth gasped as she looked into the green eyes of the person who had saved her.

"Get in the car," Conner ordered.

But Elizabeth was paralyzed—with relief, with happiness, with disbelief.

Conner! He had come for her!

The next few moments seemed like a surreal, hazy dream as Elizabeth, her body feeling numb and weightless, climbed into Conner's car and watched him as he silently drove them a safe distance from the scene of the crime.

He parked and cut the engine. His hand lingering on the gearshift, he rested his head back and closed his eyes, letting out a small sigh. Then he turned toward her. "Are you all right?" he asked.

Elizabeth had never heard his voice sound so gentle, so unaccusing. Her mouth parted open; she simply stared back at him. *Yes, I'm all right,* she thought, taking in his slightly creased forehead, his tensed square jaw, his concerned light eyes. *I'm just about perfect.*

He leaned in closer, lightly touching her arm. The feel of his fingers against her bare skin sent tingles shooting throughout her. "Are you going to be sick?" he said. "Do you need anything?" His face now came impossibly close to Elizabeth's as he leaned over and reached for something in the back of his car. She could smell his almost nonexistent aftershave; she could feel his warm breath against her neck. "I think I have a bottle of Sprite lying around here somewhere." He searched around for another minute, then shook his head. "Damn," he muttered. "I don't know where it is." He ran a hand through his short, unbrushed hair and turned back around in his seat, looking at Elizabeth.

Elizabeth's heart fluttered. He cared about her. She knew this for certain now. Whether or not he wanted to admit it, he cared about her. And that's all she needed. "Conner?" she asked softly, resting her head against his shoulder. She let out an overjoyed breath, loving the feel of his strong, sturdy frame against her cheek. "Why were you so late?"

She could feel the tension rise in his body. "What?" he asked.

"To the party," she murmured. She placed her hand flat against his stomach. She could feel his muscles through the thin cotton of his T-shirt. "You were late."

Conner put his arm around her, and her head fell against his chest. The vibrations of his speeding heartbeat matched her own racing pulse. Elizabeth closed her eyes for a moment, basking in his warmth. And the fact that he was here. For her.

Conner began to run his fingers through her hair. Elizabeth reveled in his touch. "I went to your house first," he told her in a quiet voice.

Elizabeth's heart stopped. She looked up at him. "You did?"

"Yeah. I, uh . . ." He swallowed. "I wanted to apologize for the way I acted earlier."

Goose bumps spread over every inch of Elizabeth's skin.

Conner cleared his throat. "And I wanted to thank you for being there for . . ." He looked down at the steering wheel. "Megan."

"What about you?" she asked.

"What about me?" he returned, finally lifting his gaze to look at her.

"I'm here for you too, Conner," Elizabeth whispered, lightly touching her hand to his rough cheek. "I always have been."

Conner stared back at her. *Into* her, it felt like.

"And I'm here right now," she said quietly.

Then, as a light breeze tickled Elizabeth's neck and the faint sound of sirens wailed in the nearby distance, Conner closed his eyes.

And he kissed her.

Conner McDermott

Crap. This is it. Okay, okay, I love Liz. Satisfied? There—I said it. . . . Well, yeah, okay, to myself.

But I said it.

Elizabeth Wakefield

Finally! Finally, finally, finally! Finally!